LINDA MCKOWN

I0671939

GRAY

AREA

FOR

A

WOMAN

Knight Detective Series - Book 1

BY

LINDA MCKOWN

Publisher LindaMcKownAuthor LLC

Scottsdale, AZ

GRAY AREA FOR A WOMAN

All Rights Reserved. @ 2021 by Linda McKown. No part of this publication may be reproduced or transmitted in any form or by any means, without permission in writing from the author.

Gray Area For A Woman

Knight Detective Series – Book 1

ISBN-13: 978-1-7344095-3-6

Library of Congress Control Number: 2021900007

Author:
LindaMcKownAuthor LLC
11574 E Running Deer Trail
Scottsdale, AZ 85262
https://www.lindamckown.com

Any names of people and entities are fictitious in this story having been created by the author's imagination.

Front Cover Photo of the book was purchased from Shutterstock. Book title manipulation was done by Joseph McKown

A wise person knows when to get out of the rain. There is safety under the umbrella until the lightning hits. That's when everyone with a sane mind runs for cover.

Rain comes from gray clouds when the light particles can't get through.

Enjoy a new detective series!

Table of Contents

GRAY AREA FOR A WOMAN

1 The New Detective

Detective Liam Knight watched as Hugh Farris went into their boss's office and closed the door. He wondered why there was a meeting this late in the day. The two men seemed to be in serious conversation.

Liam put his feet on his desk and tried not to stare at the glass windows into Captain Jonathan Harrison's office. He was tired from his long workday. He rubbed his hand through his brown hair and felt his shave this morning didn't work. Liam needed to buy a better shaver.

"I'll be glad to get some help on my shift."

Liam pulled up the weather map for the weekend.

"Beach temperatures seventy to ninety degrees, visibility ten miles, and satellite picture looks clear. The weather looked like another great one for LA."

The door opened and Hugh Farris stopped next to Liam's desk. Hugh's hair was thinning on top and showed new gray hair on the sides.

"The captain requests your presence."

Liam's brown eyes closed for a minute. He grabbed his badge and went into the office.

"Sit down, Liam, I have good news. Monday, Detective Penelope King will join our firm. This first week, you can show her the office and work with her on Friday. Take her out on some calls. Hugh will have her Tuesdays through Thursdays to show her the ropes on the social service side. The rest of the time she reports to you. We'll do this for a month or more and

6

see if she needs more time to get used to our routine. We're a little smaller than New York City, but we have our fair share of different problems."

Liam looked disappointed. His boss frowned.

"The last two women detectives complained about you after five months on the job before they requested a transfer. They mentioned the nut jobs weren't always on the street."

"Captain give me a break. Those women were from Texas. They didn't understand California is different. We operate with orders and rules."

His Captain believed Liam this one time.

"I want you to be nice to Penelope or else. After twenty weeks, she has options. We want her to stay. Don't hit her so hard with orders. Besides, she comes from Montana, and her dad owns a large ranch. We like powerful people. They donate money to causes important to us."

Liam understood the donation part, but he needed more information about Ms. King.

"Montana is not California. How did she ever find her way here? I get to read her file."

"No, Human Resource has been out this week. Kamilla will keep routing the work cases like she always does."

"Where did she go to school, and how long has this woman been a detective?" asked Liam.

"I believe it was upstate New York for schooling, and she worked the beat for two years in New York City before making detective. She's been a detective for a year."

Liam wasn't impressed.

"My helper is green but has an impressive daddy. Great."

Captain Harrison looked at Liam.

"She didn't ride on her old man's name to get here. Her file is impressive, and I liked her during our interview. Her specialty is working with the fire department to solve cases. We might need those skills in the future."

Liam squinted his eyes at his boss.

"We've heard some rumors about Donnie boy."

Liam shook his head in disgust. Over four million people and five hundred miles in the city of Los Angeles and this was one name he didn't expect to see soon. The greater Los Angeles area was larger and afforded more places to hide criminals.

"Crazy Donnie Corwin is in prison for five more years if I'm counting correctly."

The Captain opened his door to let Liam know the meeting was over.

"Check with some of your contacts Monday and Tuesday to see if they know anything on the streets. I don't want to call the warden at the prison without more information. Then I can make the *let's satisfy my curiosity* phone call. And Liam, try to be cheerful when you meet the recruit."

Liam left the boss and locked his desk. He looked at the busy metropolis of vehicles and people out the window. The city was his turf, and he enjoyed his work most of the time.

"Those women detectives indicated that I was a nut job. No way."

He drove to his home in the Los Angeles area which was close to the beach. Changing out of his work clothes, he jogged to the beach in a shorts outfit and sat in the sand. His phone rang.

"Becka, I'm at the beach taking a calm moment."

Becka believed today might have been a tough one. She knew the department was looking for a new detective. She hoped this one would be a young man.

He listened to her phone chatter. His girlfriend was flying out of town for a week to buy some fabric for a client's drapes. Liam wondered why the store couldn't ship the fabric. His girlfriend was going shopping for more than fabric. He would be alone for the weekend. He wasn't pleased.

"Look, I'll see you next Friday night. We'll go to a party on Saturday and celebrate your success. Don't worry, I'll be busy training a new detective next week."

He disconnected from the call and was not looking forward to Monday. The talk with his boss and Becka put him in a bad mood. Liam felt restless.

"Montana might be different than Texas. Maybe not, both states raise bulls. Montana probably has more cows than people which means more manure."

On Monday, Liam awoke late and yawned.

"Another day in paradise."

Driving to the office, he was running later than usual. He could see the tall city hall building on Spring Street.

GRAY AREA FOR A WOMAN

"Nice solid building. Finally, I've reached First Street."

Detective Penelope King was assigned the corner desk a distance away from Liam and Hugh's desk. Hugh sat around the corner. Arriving at the office, he looked over toward the recruit.

He couldn't believe the transformation. There were two stacks of in and out mailboxes on the desk. The metal boxes were stacked three feet high and large plants blocked the view of any occupant sitting in a chair. The area looked like a tropical cave.

"Oh, man, all she needs is a net with shells and coconuts. Hello, precinct, we have an introvert in the office, and she's female. I shouldn't have worried about the cows. I'm in deep trouble," said Liam to himself.

Liam watched as a delivery boy brought a large bouquet to the cave desk area.

"At least the flowers are wild."

The delivery boy disappeared. Liam wondered who ordered the batch of spring flowers for their recruit. He looked at his monitor screen for the daily schedule.

Hugh stopped by Liam's desk with his ceramic homemade cup filled with coffee. The cup was lumpy in spots.

The cup read, *Best Daddy*, sprawled awkwardly down one side.

"The detective recruit is here and appears to be a nice person. She wore her detective pin from New York City. Our pins are nicer. Too bad you were late today."

Hugh's green eyes suddenly lit up.

10

"Oh, my gosh, a new cool-guy look. You must have bought a better shaver. Maybe the haircut is working for you, too. It's a good thing you did both, because this one is a looker."

Liam was glad he spent the extra fifty dollars on the shaver.

"I was going to show her the break room. Penelope invited me into her enclave. She has placed a tremendously expensive coffee machine on her new portable table and made me a cup of gourmet coffee. I'm in seventh heaven. She buys the good stuff in those silver bags. Her plants add a little fresh ambiance to the office, don't you think?"

"Add a few coconuts and throw in a talking monkey, she should be in business to entertain the cows. Oops, no cows in LA."

Hugh looked miffed.

"You are rotten to the core, Liam. Nobody likes you. I'm sorry I complimented you and don't touch the coffee machine."

Hugh strolled away drinking his coffee.

"For a little guy, you are pretty brave."

"I heard that comment," loudly said Hugh.

Liam sniffed the air. The coffee smelled good. He looked in his desk for a new sticky note pad. The drawer fell out.

He crawled under the desk and found the large bolt which held the drawer. He put the bolt on top of his desk with the busted drawer.

One of their maintenance people brought a new office chair to the recruit's desk. Liam watched as the plastic was removed and the old chair was taken away.

He looked at his chair with dents in the foam arms and a few cut marks.

"Ms. King gets a new chair like she is royalty."

"Hey, maintenance man, my desk is falling apart."

The maintenance man ignored him. A repair ticket was required.

"What has happened to this office?"

Liam packed his bag, grabbed his badge, and sauntered over to the cave desk. The woman's back was turned. He could see she brought in her large monitor screen. Her screen was bigger. She was looking at their day's work schedule. The visual was better. He watched as she downloaded the file to her phone.

"Ms. King, I hate to interrupt, but you are scheduled to be with me today."

She turned around, and he was startled by how young she looked. Her soft long hair framed her tanned face, and her brown eyes flashed with light. She reminded him of a surfer girl he once knew. Liam bet she also jogged to stay in such good shape.

He opened his mouth to say something. He forgot the words.

"You are late," said Penelope as she wrapped her hair with a soft elastic tie.

The young woman stood, and he braced himself for the full impact. She wasn't like the other women detectives. This woman was slim with curves.

His bad mood from lack of sleep was halted for a minute.

"I ran into heavy traffic which is a common occurrence around Los Angeles. My name is Liam

Knight. You can call me Liam, and I'll try to call you Penelope unless you have a nickname."

"Penelope will be fine. I'm ready to go, Detective Knight."

"My name is Liam. Please call me by my first name."

He watched as she threw the flowers in her trash can. She saw his eyes flicker with amazement.

"They are from Marvin Edmond. He wanted to wish me luck on my first day. I don't believe in luck, nor do I like cheap daisies."

Liam blinked as she slipped past him. He talked to himself.

"Memory bank, never order any woman skimpy white daisies."

He caught up with her in the hallway. They finished the tour of the police headquarters, and Liam introduced her to the case router person named Kamilla.

"We'll check out our vehicle for the day and be on our way. Last chance for a pitstop until lunchtime."

While Penelope was in the restroom, he looked at the card on the flowers.

Call me. Good Luck! M.E.

"Well. I'll be darned, Detective King does know the District Attorney."

He crammed the card in his pocket as Penelope appeared.

"I'm ready, Liam."

"Me, too, Penelope."

He almost called her Montana. They walked to their vehicle. After a fifteen-minute drive, he stopped near a large establishment that looked like a late-night dinner place. The outside sign boasted a buffet on Sundays.

"Stay in the vehicle. This isn't a good neighborhood."

Penelope did as she was told. She input the address into her notebook.

When he returned to the car, Liam didn't tell her the reason or results of his visit which she thought was odd.

She was going to complain and thought it better to wait until the second week. At least there were no jokes about where she was from. She heard over a hundred jokes while in New York City about her home state. The bull jokes were the worst. She shouldn't have selected a hugely male profession.

2 Monday – Getting Acquainted

They drove closer to downtown LA and stopped next to what looked like a pricey nightclub. The outside was a pink and gray marble building. There were steps and brass railings. She read the sign, *Dugan's*.

"Stay here," said Liam.

Penelope frowned. She stepped out of the car and followed him up the steps. The doorman held the door open and she followed her partner. The inside of the place was elegant and richly designed with tables, booths, and a long bar. Splashes of pink, orange, and gold brightened the walls and blended well with the gray carpet. She walked past a dance floor and band area.

"Elegant tropical, the place has a nice Southern vibe."

The barman wiping the glasses spoke into a microphone, and a large man appeared in casual dress. He wore a fuchsia-colored flower shirt. From the call, she assumed the man was the owner named Dugan.

"Well, well, what have you brought me today?"

Liam was upset that his new partner was behind him.

"Detective King is a trainee. She is here to listen only."

The man put his hands on the bar.

"What is your pleasure?"

"Water sounds safe," said Penelope.

"Charge water all right with you?"

"Yes."

She sat down on the stool and accepted the charged water.

"Your necklace is beautiful," said Dugan.

"Thank you."

Liam frowned. All he saw was a white gold chain.

"You have some information. I called you on Saturday."

Dugan handed the detective a piece of paper with a name and address.

"Donnie Corwin's sister has moved several times. My people tracked her down. She's probably home now. The woman works evenings at a greasy hamburger place. Rumor is they sell joints on the side."

Liam took the note. He would have to turn in the marijuana problem. He signaled to Penelope that they were leaving. She gulped down her water and waved to Dugan who watched her like a hawk as she left.

When they reached the car, he stopped and looked at Penelope.

"When I tell you to do something, I expect you to obey. I told you to stay in the car. As your trainer, you are required to listen, or we don't get along."

Penelope stepped into the car and slammed her door shut. Liam raised his eyebrows but didn't respond. He remembered his boss telling him to go easy on the orders and to be cheerful.

When they reached the small, dilapidated house, Liam knocked on the door. A woman with a freckled face and graying red hair answered the door.

He introduced themselves to the overweight woman in tight clothes. She picked up a large bag of cookies and ate two.

"We've heard rumors that Donnie might have a deal to shorten his time. I know you might have heard the same thing."

The woman put the third cookie on the coffee table with the bag and started complaining.

"What am I going to do? They shouldn't release him. All he will do is start another fire. This time, he might hurt people. First, he'll come to me and take all my money. There should be free police protection."

Liam looked at Penelope and shook his head. She knew not to interfere.

"Where did you hear about Donnie getting a deal?"

Ms. Corwin sniffled.

"There are people I know at the prison. The wives of the other prisoners talk to the other women who visit. We have connected, and some of us are good friends on social media. Donnie bragged about the deal, and said he was going to be out real soon."

"How soon?"

"Probably a month or two is what he told people."

"Thank you, Ms. Corwin. I think you should be fine for now. Once Donnie is released, I'll ask my boss if the blues can step up patrols in your area."

They left the home, reached their vehicle, and Liam drove to a nearby shopping center.

"The large store has restrooms and sandwiches in the food court."

They went inside. Penelope was delighted by the Asian-style salad. They took their orders to a nearby table and ate.

"Who is this Donnie Corwin?"

Liam ate a bite out of his roast beef sandwich.

"Too bland but they put in lots of meat."

He took a packet of horseradish sauce out of his jacket pocket. Liam squeezed the stuff on the inside and took a bite.

"This is better."

He stopped talking. Penelope was looking at the empty packet.

"Dugan keeps a dish of the packets in the refrigerator at the bar for me. Getting back to Corwin, he is one bad dude. Being in prison all these years hasn't helped us. He now has technical skills to enhance his abilities to start a fire."

Penelope stuck her fork in her salad.

"Who put Donnie away?"

Liam looked off in the distance.

"Dodge has retired. He was one of our senior detectives who caught the man. You might get to meet him. I was the other person on the team. I'm sure Donnie hates our office as much as we hate him."

She stopped chewing her salad and swallowed.

"You'll need my help."

Liam wasn't sure her youth and inexperience would help. She was waiting for his agreement.

"Yes, detective."

He saw her pink diamond heart necklace.

"Who gave you the diamond?"

Liam took a sip of his cola drink.

"My dad. He calls me Pink."

Spitting out the ice in his mouth, he burst out laughing. Using the napkin, he wiped up the ice.

"Sorry. You said Pink. Now that is cute. Your initials are P.K. so I get the nickname. I like the name much better than Montana."

"My partner should respect me and keep my father's name for me quiet. The guys at the last office were terrible about my name, especially around Valentine's Day. My entire desk and chair were covered with pink stickies. They even put them on the floor in the shape of Montana. Please keep calling me Penelope."

Liam tossed his wrapper and grabbed her empty salad bowl. After garbage was dispensed with, they headed toward the office. He needed to talk with their boss.

"I'll submit today's report. You can help me do Friday's report. Tomorrow is when Hugh Farris will take over."

"Hugh seems nice."

Liam looked skeptical.

"Hugh and I walk on thin ice. He doesn't like me or my current dating habits. He believes I'm difficult for any female to be around. Hugh is wrong. I'm right. His wife, Emma, is extremely sociable. She likes me. She will invite you to dinner. You should go. She is an excellent cook and keeps their kids in line."

Penelope was silent thinking about her day tomorrow. Everything was new again which was what she wanted. Her past was too painful. She was used to detectives being at odds, especially the males.

"Ego problem."

"You are so right. Hugh has a huge ego."

Liam put a recorded CD in the car player and selected a song. They slowed to their next exit which was two miles away.

"Gridlock. This ought to take ten minutes. How did you get a new chair?"

"I asked for one."

"You wouldn't have a screwdriver in your desk?"

"No."

He started singing the tune on the CD. Penelope joined in, singing the alternate parts. Liam was surprised she knew the song and commented.

"Nice voice. You know the words."

"In Montana, there isn't much to do other than watch the buffalo and cows. We learned all the old songs."

"Buffalo and cows are two words you never hear in LA. Bulls run third. Any cowboys left behind?"

Penelope laughed.

"There may be a dozen."

Liam was surprised at the revelation.

"The count would have been higher only my dad scared them off."

He chuckled.

"And your mom?"

"She orders my clothes whenever she visits. Dresses, usually."

"What about your parents?" asked Penelope.

"Gone. I'm okay with being alone."

This first day with the new detective surprised him. Liam knew Hugh was correct. The woman was likable. Then he remembered she didn't obey an order. He would need to fix that problem.

"Why all the plants?"

Penelope didn't know if she should answer. She was still seeing a therapist after two months off.

"The greenery helps. They are part of the save-the-earth and humankind project."

"You don't look like a person who joins movements of any kind. Humans create trash and smog. Saving the earth gets harder."

"Your view is cynical and possibly correct. I don't have the time for volunteering. The florist gives money to the needy in her community when people buy ferns. I'm helping some," said Penelope.

Liam pulled into the headquarters parking lot for the vehicle return. Penelope gathered her things and disappeared to the employee parking lot. He looked over the railing and watched her drive a silver-gray sports car and turn north.

"At least Pink likes nice cars."

Liam texted his boss who left for the day.

"I'll send my report from home."

Liam stepped into his black sports car and drove home. He also headed north and turned west to the beach.

"Penelope. Interesting woman. This car is impressive."

He stepped on the gas and rubbed his face. The new shaver was better.

3 Second Day at Work – Person Missing

Hugh Farris looked at another newly arrived bouquet. This one was tiny pink roses that sat on Penelope's desk. He smelled the tiny buds and read the card.

Still waiting, Edmond.

"Edmond? I know only one person with that name in Los Angeles. This can't be the District Attorney again?"

Hugh tucked the card back and tiptoed to his desk around the corner. Carter watched him strangely. Hugh pointed at his empty cup. Carter nodded. Hugh was waiting for Penelope to offer him some more fresh coffee.

Swatting at a fly on his desk, Hugh wondered how the fly reached their floor. Usually, the boys on the second floor killed them with bug spray. He glanced at his watch. He wasn't worried about Detective Carter.

Penelope was on time.

Hugh waited until he smelled coffee. Getting up, he was surprised to see Liam standing at her desk blocking his way. Hugh frowned.

"Detective King is supposed to go with me today," mentioned Hugh.

Liam turned.

"There's been a change. The boss wants the three of us in his office pronto. My fingerprints were removed from the coffee machine."

"Oh, great, we have a department meeting?"

"The meeting is only us, not the whole department."

The three detectives went into Captain Harrison's office. The room was large and organized. The desk was mahogany, and the chair was a plush navy-blue leather. A navy and red-colored rug were on the floor. There were framed pictures on the wall of honorary degrees and awards. He motioned to the three copies on his desk. The detectives selected a copy of a report of a missing person. Hugh quickly scanned the file.

"Are you kidding me? Duane Hicks is missing. Go figure that one. He's probably stuck on the eighth green at the golf course testing the wind direction. If he is missing, I'm sure his wife will be delighted," said Hugh.

"The reason that I asked you to attend the meeting is this disappearance might take a while to resolve. In three weeks, Liam goes on vacation, and Hugh will need to fill in for Liam that week."

Hugh nodded. He knew Liam and his girlfriend were going to Greece for a holiday together. With Liam out of the office, things should be peaceful.

"No problem. I can work with Penelope while Liam has lots of fun in Greece with Becka."

Penelope slid a glance at Liam who was still reading the file. He looked up at her. She quickly glanced away. The detective told her he was okay with being alone. A girlfriend wasn't exactly alone status.

"I'll talk to the police that turned in the missing case and see if there's more information. I will get an appointment with Beverly Hicks this week," commented Liam.

Harrison nodded.

"The twenty-million-dollar life insurance policy on Duane doesn't look good. There needs to be a body for them to pay the claim quickly. Currently, we have none."

Penelope spoke, "She waited exactly twenty-four hours before she reported her husband missing."

Hugh piped up, "Mrs. Hicks was five minutes early according to the call record. She called on Tuesday which is the day her pool guy comes around. My wife has heard rumors about marital discord. You never know about rumors."

Jonathan handed Penelope a small box. She opened and saw her gold Los Angeles detective pin.

"There's also a detective badge."

He slid the badge across his desk toward her.

"Thank you, Captain."

Liam stood, and they filed out of the boss's office. Hugh and Penelope went to the cave and filled their mugs with coffee. Liam came over and held out his cup. Penelope poured the last coffee from the pot. He saw the tiny roses in the garbage.

"Thanks for the coffee, Pink. Mental note, no cheap wild or tiny flowers."

Liam walked away.

Hugh looked oddly at Liam and turned.

"Don't pay any attention to him. His bad side shows ninety percent of the time. This is your space, including the coffee pot and garbage can."

"Thanks, I'll remember."

She put her detective pin in her desk drawer. She decided to wear her old pin the first week. The old pin was familiar. The badge went in her jacket pocket. She was official.

Hugh and Penelope found their vehicle to use for the day. Hugh drove to a large red-orange brick building.

"We have kiddie duty today. I tried to get out of this job, but they are shorthanded at the social worker's office. The blues have a department meeting. Kamilla didn't listen to me. I told her Carter didn't look busy."

"I'm sure everything will be all right. I've done the junior thing. Carter skipped out when he saw Kamilla approaching his desk."

Hugh ground his teeth together over Carter.

"Watch everything in this car, and this young lady's name is Colleen Brewster. She's a piece of work and is dangerous. Something sets her off. All we have to do is deliver her to the psychiatrist, wait until her appointment is over, and return her to the detention facility."

"Should I unbuckle my gun?"

"Good grief, no. She's not hardcore dangerous. But we might have to run after her."

"Colleen sounds delightful."

Hugh snorted. Two guards brought the young woman to their vehicle and placed her inside. They shut the door quickly. Hugh introduced Penelope. Penelope looked at the woman with curly hair and deadpan eyes. She buckled her seatbelt, and the car pulled away from the curb.

25

GRAY AREA FOR A WOMAN

Penelope tried to make light conversation with the young woman. Her hair was short and long like she cut the hair herself.

"Colleen, where do you come from?"

There was no response. Penelope saw a medic bracelet on the young woman's wrist.

"She's originally from Santa Monica but her mom moved to Pomona a year ago. That's when she got into lots of trouble messing with her drugs."

Penelope shook her head.

"Drugs will mess with a person."

Hugh corrected himself.

"She forgets to take her prescription drugs which results in problems. Also, she's a little hard of hearing. She can talk when she wants. Most of the time Colleen is abrupt. She's into the teenager phase called play dumb."

"What's with the bracelet?"

"Colleen is allergic to bees."

The young woman in the back seat talked.

"Hot and stingy."

"I didn't see her medication pen. What if she gets stung while she is with us?"

"There's one in the glove compartment if we need to help her."

Penelope checked the glove compartment to make sure.

"Shouldn't she carry one?"

Hugh knew the answer.

"They are training her on how to use one. Things are going slow. She's resisting."

"Does she require special schooling because of the hearing?"

Hugh wasn't sure.

"I think she used to go to regular school. Since arriving in Pomona, I don't know. She might do her homework online."

The rest of the ride to the psychiatrist's office was quiet. More guards escorted Colleen into the doctor's office. They sat down in some chairs and waited. Colleen disappeared with the guards and a receptionist.

In forty-five minutes, the guards escorted Colleen back to the car and locked her inside. Penelope was glad there was a cage between the young woman and the detectives.

Colleen's face and frown grew deeper the closer they came to the detention facility. They were ten minutes away when the young woman began drawing images on the windows and car seats with a red tube of lipstick.

Hugh sighed.

"Not again. Colleen, you need to stop. Put the lipstick down."

"How did she get lipstick?"

The young woman didn't listen. He made the call to the detention facility. When they pulled up, there were two guards with a doctor with a syringe waiting for them. As soon as the door was opened, Colleen made a run for it. The guards caught her. The drug was administered, and they escorted the young woman inside.

Penelope watched Hugh.

GRAY AREA FOR A WOMAN

"We return the car to the lot and get a new one. Last month she had a razor blade in her hand which was worse. There was a fly in the car. She went into a kill zone."

Penelope swallowed.

"Maybe Colleen needs a new psychiatrist. This one isn't working."

Hugh was surprised by the comment.

"I'll mention your insightful recommendation to the social worker. There is a problem."

Hugh put his sunglasses on.

"Liam called you, Pink?"

She watched as he parked the car.

"My dad calls me that name. I made the mistake of telling my other partner. He choked on his ice."

Hugh turned over the car to the waiting attendant.

"There's a sandwich shop not far from here. Let's walk and eat lunch before we finish our day."

They stopped at the deli. She ordered a salad with beans and cheese. Hugh ordered a ham sandwich.

"I assume Liam is going to Greece with his girlfriend. Becka is a female name," said Penelope.

"Yes. He's been dating Becka Smith for about fourteen months now. She's a real record for Liam. Usually, the man switches girlfriends out a lot earlier. I don't think he wants to go to Greece. He's been frowning a lot."

Penelope opened her bag of breadsticks and took a bite.

"You don't like Liam very much?"

Hugh smeared mustard on his ham.

"Don't get me wrong, he is a good detective. Let me correct myself; he is a smart detective. Instincts up the wazoo. Sometimes the way he gets things done seems off-the-wall. Yet, he puts the culprits away. The Captain knows his detectives. I think how he treats women is wrong."

She ate some beans and cheese.

"The Captain likes Liam. You are warning me to be careful."

Hugh smiled.

"You're wise to office politics. Don't fall for Liam's charm."

"I'm not going there. Charm doesn't work since age sixteen. I prefer real feelings, and I've given up dating detectives."

"Good girl."

4 DA Visit and Beverly Hicks

Liam honked his horn at the driver that cut in front of him. He looked at his watch which showed he was fifteen minutes late as he pulled into the parking lot. Entering the building and taking three steps at a time in the stairways, he reached his desk in a minute.

Working out with the gym equipment at his home and jogging the beach kept him in excellent physical shape.

Looking toward Penelope's desk, he was surprised to see a tall man in a business suit talking with her. Liam knew who the man was visiting with his detective trainee.

Turning on his computer, Liam downloaded the work schedule for today. He left a slot open for the interview with Beverly Hicks. Carter wasn't anywhere around. Liam crawled underneath his desk and fixed his drawer. Satisfied, he walked over to Penelope's desk. A fresh bouquet of yellow tulips laid on her desk in clear plastic.

"The coconut is missing."

Marvin turned around.

"Excuse me, Mr. Edmond, my partner and I have a meeting scheduled with Mrs. Duane Hicks, and we need to leave."

The District Attorney wondered about the coconut comment.

"Detective Knight, I was wrapping up my conversation with Penelope. Her father and I are old friends. We both golf."

The DA touched Penelope's shoulder tenderly.

"Good day, Penelope. I look forward to seeing you at the garden party this weekend."

Liam raised his eyebrows. Penelope let Marvin leave. She watched over her ferns until he exited the room. Quickly she threw the limp tulips in the garbage.

She stepped past her partner and headed to the garage.

Liam shouldn't have been taken aback.

"Pour tulips. I guess she doesn't like yellow either. Mental note, no yellow flowers with limp stems."

Liam followed her out of headquarters. He signed for their vehicle and stepped inside. Turning the key, the engine started. He waited. Penelope stepped inside.

"I needed some air."

"No problem, two minutes of air helps a person breathe better."

He drove toward the freeway. The traffic was heavy this time of day. Liam expertly moved forward. They drove into the Hollywood area of homes and stopped at a large gate. Penelope read the sign of the housing community. The security guard let them pass. They drove past large lawns and pricey homes. Some of the mansions showed massive private gates.

Liam imagined all the cool cars were in the large, air-conditioned garages.

"Let me ask the questions. I've known the Hicks for some time. We run into each other at the same parties."

Penelope figured there was a connection. He noticed her quiet mood.

"My girlfriend is an interior designer. She has lots of rich clients. She's done drapes for Beverly in her den. Beverly ripped out perfectly good wooden blinds. Why don't you tell Mr. Edmond that you don't like flowers?"

Penelope saw manicured lawns. Their car stopped at a large rambling brick ranch home with a huge fountain.

"I love flowers."

She stepped out of the car and went to the front door.

"You could have fooled me," said Liam.

He joined her and rang the doorbell. A butler led them to a library. They waited for Beverly to arrive.

"Liam, what a pleasant surprise? I thought Hugh was coming to interview me. You're much better looking."

"Beverly, we do have questions. I visited your husband's sailboat, and the police found his car in the parking lot. The parking lot camera showed he left the Ventura Harbor around eight in the evening and returned at nine to his boat. From there, we have no other information. According to the police report, he called you before eight last Friday evening and told you he was staying overnight."

The butler brought a tray of tea. Liam and Penelope declined.

"That was the last I heard from him. We were going to eat dinner on Saturday, but he never showed. Duane wouldn't miss dinner. Not that he talks to me.

His golf cronies are important. I called the police because I was worried. They haven't found him. He would have called me by now."

Liam frowned. He knew Beverly only worried about money and her next hair appointment.

"Why didn't you check out his sailboat?"

Beverly sat down.

"We haven't exactly been sociable lately. We talked about the divorce word. If he was on the boat, I didn't want a confrontation."

Penelope stopped looking at the paintings in the room and glanced at Liam.

"Is there any other place besides the country club and the golf course where Duane might stay?"

"We do own a ski chalet in Squaw Valley. The manager checked our place, and there was no sign of Duane. The manager told me our freezer light was blinking. There's nothing in the separate freezer. He unplugged the thing. I needed Duane to handle the repair."

Liam wrote down the ski place's home address.

"If you can think of any other place your husband might have gone, let us know. Perhaps he decided to take a mini-vacation."

Beverly laughed.

"I doubt it. The man is a workaholic and very shrewd. He purchased a life insurance policy on me also."

Penelope's eyes darkened. Something didn't seem right. She asked the question.

"Is your policy the same amount?"

Liam frowned at his partner.

"Heavens no, my policy is for thirty million."

"Really."

Beverly sighed.

"I make more money than my husband. Hence, my worth is higher."

"Does anyone know about these policies besides your lawyer?"

The woman thought about the question.

"You know how things go at a party. Of course, we talk with our friends and joke about things. There's no harm making fun of who's worth more."

Mrs. Hicks rose to signal she was done talking.

"Tell Becka hello for me. I hear she did a splendid job on the Andersen's living room."

Liam smiled.

"I will. Goodbye."

The two detectives left and drove to Ventura Harbor. They walked into the outdoor barbeque area. Penelope sat while Liam brought their fried fish and chicken. Squeezing a heavy dose of the light-colored barbeque sauce on his fried fish, Liam took a bite.

"The barbeque sauce is for the fish?" asked Penelope.

"Try the sauce. There's light mustard, lemon, a touch of brown sugar, mayo, sour cream, and apple cider vinegar with herbs."

Penelope put a tiny bit of sauce on her fish and took a bite. She was surprised.

"I told you the sauce was good. Now you believe me. After we're done, I'll show you Mr. Hicks's sailboat."

"What if someone overheard Mr. or Mrs. Hicks talk about their life insurance policies?"

"My feelings are disclosure about private matters isn't a wise move."

"A lover might be a problem."

Liam understood. They walked to a long dock and found the boat. He brought out a key, and they went inside.

"Mrs. Hicks gave me the key."

There was beer in the refrigerator and no food. The garbage can was empty. The bed was made, and the bathroom was clean.

"The man seems to be overly neat. He made his bed and took out the garbage. The inside is clean, and the outside surfaces washed and polished."

They walked outside. While Liam locked the sailboat, Penelope looked around. Some men were washing a motorboat further down.

The sailboat next to the Hicks's boat looked neglected. The sail cover was dusty and the ties that showed the wind direction were frayed. There were some leaves on the floor. The windows on this side were shut.

"Let's talk to the cleaning boys," said Penelope as she moved forward.

They walked down to the men. She glanced at Duane Hicks's boat. This side's windows were shut. Penelope talked with the boat cleaners. She took their business card, and they returned to their vehicle.

"Did anyone contact the derelict boat owner next to the Hicks's?"

"I did. His name is Mason Jarett. He's about sixty-three years old. He broke his leg some time ago and was not able to get his boat cleaned for the season. Mason mentioned that he hasn't seen Duane since last year."

Penelope watched the ocean water as he drove.

"Thoroughly cleaning a boat takes money. He might be shelving the cost. Where are we going?"

"There's a boat repair place that Duane always uses. I thought we might want to find out any last repairs that were done to his boat, and when they saw him last."

Liam talked with the boat repair manager and returned to the car.

"The boat was hauled out, scraped of barnacles, and repainted on the bottom last year. They also did a tune-up on the engine and replaced some lines. Lines are ropes to the land lovers in this world. He said the sailboat was in tiptop shape for this summer."

Penelope was right. The man took care of the things he loved. The sailboat was something Duane wanted in his life. He wasn't taking good care of his relationship with his wife.

"The sailboat is more important than the wife."

Liam glanced at her.

"Interesting observation. Duane does like to sail. Beverly used to go with him. She stopped about a year ago. Currently, she spends her time at the mall and her pool. We checked her credit cards. She likes Saturday morning sales."

"Do you think the man did disappear?"

Liam pulled over.

"The question is self-explanatory. We have an official document stating the man is missing. No one has seen him."

Penelope felt strange.

"There is a strangeness to this case. I read the police report. The wife is lying. I think she checked the sailboat. Someone only needed to drop her off, and she could avoid the parking lot cameras. Plus, her husband might have taken a break from his marriage and skipped town."

Liam knew Beverly. She wasn't always truthful.

"I think you might be right regarding both ideas. Beverly lied. She hated the Ralph Andersen living room. The red carpet was not a favorite. Duane might have skipped town."

"Who puts red on their floor?"

Liam shook his head.

"People with money. Next year, the carpet might be purple. Money provides the ability to change things and hides a lot of flaws."

"Where do we go from here on the missing person investigation?"

Liam pulled back into traffic.

"We look for a body which moves or doesn't move."

They returned to the office.

"My parents are visiting this weekend. Our boss let me take Monday off. I'm supposed to let you know."

Liam wasn't upset.

"Have fun at your garden party with your folks and the DA."

GRAY AREA FOR A WOMAN

"We will."

Penelope was glad her first week was over. She hadn't expected her parents to show up so soon.

"Thanks. They arrived earlier than planned."

Liam nodded.

"You must be an only child."

She looked at him and smiled.

"Guilty."

"Watch yourself with the District Attorney. He is getting a divorce. The wife wants the house in Malibu, and he won't give her the place. The house is in a perfect setting and close to their friends."

Penelope already knew about the situation.

"We are friends, and I know about their current problem. Too bad they can't work things out."

Liam watched her walk away.

"I don't think three bouquets equate to a friend. The guy is in hot pursuit to find another female. He just has poor taste in flowers."

Liam ran into Hugh in the hall next to Hugh's desk.

"Any update on Hicks?"

"No, other than Penelope thinks he takes better care of his boat."

Hugh scrunched up his face.

"I told you that she was intelligent and better than your last two detectives. I saw she killed the tulips. They look prettier in the ground."

"For once, Hugh, you make a lot of sense."

Hugh was glad they were back to being friends.

"I saw you fixed the desk drawer. Can I borrow your electric screwdriver?"

"No."

"Oh, Liam, come on. I thought we were friends. I've got an outside light problem."

Liam looked at the man.

"You always have an outside light problem. Get a bigger electrical box or have the electrician install new outlets."

"Those are expensive," yelled Hugh.

Liam didn't hear him or was ignoring him as he walked away.

Hugh went on the internet and called an electrician.

"I need an estimate."

5 Daytime Garden Party

Penelope's mom helped her with the zipper on her new dress.

"Thank you for the dresses. I guess my closet isn't too exciting."

Her mother shook her head.

"You can't wear shorts and sweats to a party. Where did your other dresses go?"

"When I moved, the old dresses and heels went to the thrift store. I didn't think I needed them here. There were no plans for parties or dating."

Her father knocked.

"Come in, Warren, dear. We women are dressed. At least our daughter now has three perfectly elegant dresses in her closet. I'm glad we stopped at the shopping center yesterday to get dresses and shoes. I told you Penelope was impossible. She had no plans to go to parties."

Her father chuckled.

"Wendy, and Pink, let's get moving. We have a party on our agenda. I'm hungry plus I will be glad to talk with some old friends. Although I heard our friend, Marvin Edmond, has been sending our daughter flowers. Are you dating?"

Penelope looked exasperated that Marvin told him. Now she would need to explain.

"Warren King, we agreed to leave our daughter alone about dating. No pushing."

"Then, why did you buy three dresses when she only needs one for this party?"

"Mom, I'm all right with the question. We are only friends. He was trying to help me feel welcome to Los Angeles. Who is having a garden party?"

"Mr. and Mrs. Ralph Andersen."

Penelope remembered the name.

"She redecorated her living room."

Her mother grabbed their small clutches and handed Penelope her silver bag which matched the silver chiffon dress.

"When she shows us the room, don't gasp."

"Never," said Penelope.

"Our limousine rental has arrived. Shall we ladies?"

They went to the Andersen compound and were dropped off at the front terrace which was already filled with guests. Marvin saw them and immediately came over. He shook her father's hand.

"Warren and Wendy King, I'm delighted you have arrived. The list of guests is long. Good thing they staggered the times on the invitations. Let me show you where the champagne is located."

Marvin touched Penelope on her lower back and gave her a quick kiss.

"You look awesome in gray."

"I believe the color is silver."

"Whatever color you wear makes you look beautiful."

"Thanks."

A man across the lawn watched the group of people drinking champagne. Becka approached him.

"I'll be about fifteen or twenty more minutes. Then we can leave."

GRAY AREA FOR A WOMAN

Liam looked at his date. His girlfriend timed their arrival to mingle with the important guests. The King group was running a little late.

"Don't worry. I'll wait here and people watch."

He was impressed that Penelope's parents knew the Andersen's. The estate was huge and in an extremely rich neighborhood. He watched as Marvin either held Penelope's arm or touched her back.

"She only let you kiss her once, and she's trying to keep her distance. Not as friendly as I thought toward the DA. Great dress."

Hugh approached Liam.

"I thought I saw you from the food area. This lunch spread is the best. They have lobster, calamari, clams, and shrimp. My wife couldn't make the party, but I came because I thought I should mingle with a better group of society. That's why I was shocked you were here."

Liam drank his drink. He was used to Hugh's dry humor.

"Glad to see you, too. Guess who else made the party?"

Hugh looked across the lawn. He groaned.

"The DA is here. I should have known."

Hugh turned so no one could see him. Liam stirred the lime in his ginger ale. The people on the grounds appeared happy, and the conversations were lively.

"I've asked a few people if they've seen Duane Hicks or know what he was up to before he disappeared."

"There is a gleam in your eye which tells me something interesting popped up."

Liam took a sip and crunched on the ice. He squeezed the juice out of the lime slice.

"He was planning a trip south on the water to Mexico with a girl he met recently. Duane kept talking about a three-week sailing trip. He told his friends three girls were paying him for the trip plus the young woman."

"Why would Duane take money for a trip? Four women onboard sound like a heap of trouble. There's only one bathroom. We should interview the other boat owners. Sometimes people take pictures when they have boat parties. There might be pictures of this mystery girl or the other women."

Liam looked at Penelope's group. They were moving toward the food tents.

"I know. Duane doesn't need money. Monday is when I'll check their financials. Good idea about interviewing the other Ventura boat people. Thanks, Hugh."

Hugh looked at the crowd of people on the lawn.

"Not too many cops here."

"You missed the security people. They have a tent at the back of the pool house. Penelope's parents are here visiting."

"Life is amazing. Security people get their special tent. We don't ever get tents," complained Hugh.

GRAY AREA FOR A WOMAN

"The King family is at the Andersen party. I saw them from a distance. They were walking toward the food court with the DA. Penelope is in a silver dress."

"Penelope and her parents are here? I thought you were pulling my leg."

Liam caught Hugh at a disadvantage.

"They are on the grounds. I've got to run. Becka is signaling me that she is ready to leave."

Hugh watched the detective join his girlfriend, Becka. Hugh waved. Then he walked toward the food tent.

"A couple more pieces of shrimp and lobster can't hurt. I can meet Penelope's parents. This party is a winner all the way around. I wonder how many acres the King family own in Montana. The house is probably small. Tread lightly. I'm sure they would prefer their daughter home and not working as a detective in crazy Los Angeles."

Penelope saw Hugh coming and disconnected from Marvin.

"Hello, Hugh, good timing. This party is lovely. Let me introduce you to my parents, Wendy, and Warren King. You already know Mr. Edmond."

Hugh shook their hands, and they talked up a storm about types of cows and which ones worked for Montana winters.

"I didn't know the depth of fur on a cow was important," said Hugh.

Penelope was relieved as her parents seemed to enjoy themselves. Hugh talked about how he and Detective Knight were helping Penelope learn the ropes.

"She's brilliant and makes good coffee. I'm sorry you didn't get to meet Liam. He was here with his girlfriend, Becka."

Penelope was shocked. She didn't see them. She wondered why Liam didn't come over to visit with her parents. After an hour, Hugh left them.

Her father took Wendy's hand.

"We need to thank our guests and leave. Good seeing you again, Marvin."

Marvin whispered to Penelope, "I'll call you after your parents leave, and you should look for a huge bouquet on Tuesday."

Before she could tell him not to send any more flowers, Marvin was gone.

"I hope he doesn't send funeral flowers," said Penelope.

She didn't like gladiolas, especially coral. Her dad motioned for her to move up the steps to the main patio.

"Having fun? Hugh likes your detective skills."

"Sure, dad. Your friends have also put on a nice party."

"You and the District Attorney seemed to hit things off today. I know I'm not supposed to mention men."

She screwed up her face. He saw her look.

"A father can always hope. I did like Hugh. He's older and fun. The Liam person sounds like a challenge."

"Liam is a tough guy."

"I like tough. We should meet sometime." Warren took his wife's arm.

GRAY AREA FOR A WOMAN

Penelope shrugged. She followed her parents to greet the party's owners. She wasn't sure her parents should meet Liam.

LINDA MCKOWN

6 Second Week – Dry-cleaner Shop

Penelope rushed to work on Tuesday. She was twelve minutes late. Prickles of sweat showed on her brow. The traffic from the airport was terrible. At least her parents were on a flight returning to Billings, Montana. She heaved a sigh of relief.

Liam was glancing her way with a smile on his face. She hated his smug look.

Penelope turned to her desk and stopped dead in her tracks. She groaned.

"Oh, no. I can't believe this is happening. An evil witch is interfering with my life."

She tapped her fingers to her forehead. Grabbing a tissue, she wiped her sweaty face and tossed the tissue. Pulling the metal garbage can out from under her desk, she shoved her chair into the hallway.

One by one she pulled coral-colored gladiolas out of the foam urn and dumped the stems in her garbage can. Hurriedly, she shoved her chair back and grabbed the large urn. Water spilled on her jacket.

"Nuts."

She handed the urn to the closest person she could find.

"Carter, please dispose of this for me. Watch out; there's water inside. I've got to meet Hugh."

"Sure thing, Penelope. Did you need the card which is stuck to the urn? How about my handkerchief? You are all wet."

"No! Dump it. My jacket will air dry."

Liam watched as Penelope went out the back door to the parking lot.

He sat on the edge of Carter's desk.

"Let me take care of the vase for you. I'm going to the men's room."

"Gee, I appreciate your help. Did you see how wet her jacket was? I didn't want to tell her the flower food might stain."

"I did see the jacket, but we probably shouldn't remind her. She's had a tough weekend with her parents here. There was a party with the DA at the Andersen's."

"Right," said Carter. He disappeared whenever the District Attorney appeared in the office.

Liam took the urn to the restroom and peeled off the card. There was no one in the men's stalls. He read the card.

Loved the silver dress. Dinner, my place? ME.

Liam threw the vase in the trash. He walked past Penelope's desk before he went to a boat at Ventura Harbor to talk to a boat owner who had some pictures. He saw the gladiolas.

"Mental note, she hates coral."

Liam texted Hugh that he might have a lead on Hicks's ladies.

Hugh let Penelope drive because the car fan worked on her side of the car. The jacket was still damp. He read his text.

"Your suit should be dry by the time we get to the grocery store. However, you might want to drop the jacket off at the nearest cleaners."

Penelope looked in the car mirror and saw the green tinge growing larger. Her eyes grew wide. The suit jacket was expensive.

"The grocery store owner has this ten or twelve-year-old kid that comes in every week. The kid steals a loaf of bread and a small jar of peanut butter. I think we might have a case of a negligent parent. That's why we got the call."

Penelope parked the car a distance from the front door of the grocery store. They walked inside and talked with the owner. He didn't know who the child was nor the parents.

Hugh finished his notes.

"We might as well grab some chips and bottled water for a snack."

They wandered down to the coolers. Penelope saw a kid enter the store in the overhead mirror.

"Look, we just got lucky. This might be the little thief."

"Go out the back and I'll circle to the front. He'll run your way. Handcuff him if you have to get him to stop or trip him."

The kid went for the bread and peanut butter. Hugh was outside the front door with his badge. The kid ran to the back. Penelope put out her foot, and the kid went flying into a large, stacked pile of canned vegetables. The bread and peanut butter hit the wall.

"A lady cop in this store is weird. Why did you trip me?"

Penelope quickly put a plastic tie on his hands because the handcuffs were too large. She picked the kid off the floor and took him to the front of the store.

GRAY AREA FOR A WOMAN

"Women aren't weird."

Hugh found out the kid's home address. Penelope paid for the crushed bread and broken-lidded peanut butter jar. The seal was intact. They put the kid in the back of the car and drove to his home. Hugh knocked on the door.

A woman came running outside.

"Why do you have my child tied up? I'm going to sue the two officers in front of me."

Hugh explained the ongoing theft for the last eight weeks to the mother. Once she realized what was happening, she waved them inside.

"I lost my job and have been doing odd jobs like ironing for the neighbors. I'm getting evicted next month. Missy, you should get your jacket cleaned."

"I know. Flower water isn't good for cloth with woven fibers."

Hugh stepped out of the house and made a call to social services. Penelope made a call to the grocery store after looking inside the refrigerator.

The social service person and the delivery boy arrived at the same time. Penelope took the box of groceries into the kitchen with the boy. He helped put away the milk, butter, cold cheese, deli hotdogs, and ice cream. Next, they put away canned goods, cereal, and bread.

"Why is my mom talking to the person in the other room and Detective Farris? We appreciate the food."

"Social services can help your mom until she gets a new job. This food is temporary. They will set up food delivery or let your mom know where to go. You won't have to steal anymore."

The boy was silent.

"Can I try the ice cream?"

"Sure."

The boy brought out bowls, a scoop, and spoons.

"I only want a tiny scoop," said Penelope.

The boy's eyes bulged.

"I thought everybody liked ice cream."

"Sorry, I'm not a real fan. Hey, vanilla is the best, but just a little."

The young boy finally smiled.

"My name is Randi Sanford."

She held out her hand.

"Detective Penelope King."

"My mom yells at me when I get my clothes wet. There's an excellent dry-cleaner next to Bonnie's haircut place. People say he is a wizard with stains."

When Hugh was done, he came into the kitchen.

"I missed ice cream. Oh, darn. I guess I'll wait until we get back to the station. Ready, Detective King?"

"Yes."

She turned to Randi.

"Take care of your mom."

"I will."

The two detectives left and drove to a beauty parlor. Penelope told Hugh she was going to see if the dry-cleaner could clean her jacket in an hour.

GRAY AREA FOR A WOMAN

Hugh went inside the beauty parlor and talked with the woman about Randi Sanford's mom. Penelope joined him minus her jacket.

"Randi's mom needs a part-time job until the real job comes through."

Hugh handed the woman named Bonnie a piece of paper with the woman's name and phone number.

"I'll give Mrs. Sanford a call after you leave. We can use extra help with cleaning, reloading supplies, and the lobby area. My girls are swamped with business."

"Thanks, Bonnie, for helping a neighbor. Her son, Randi, could also help with garbage detail and stocking."

"Don't worry. We take care of our own."

They left, found a tea shop, and waited until the dry-cleaner man called.

"Thirty minutes. The man told me he would get the job done. He saw my New York pin."

Hugh and Penelope left to pick up the jacket. Her jacket was cleaned, restored, and like new. She hung the plastic bag in the back of the car.

"The dry-cleaner guy is a wizard."

While driving, he called his wife, Emma, about dinner. After he hung up, Hugh turned to his partner.

"My wife said she can do dinner this Thursday evening. You are officially invited after work. No fancy dress is required. She's making a pot roast with vegetables."

"I would love to come. I'll need your address and what type of wine to bring."

"Anything red and I'll text our address to you."

Penelope was quiet until they returned to headquarters. She exited the car and grabbed the plastic dry-cleaner bag.

"Today was interesting."

Hugh agreed with her.

"We do have a problem on Thursday. Colleen has an appointment with a new psychiatrist. We get to take her there. Carter is taking a day of vacation."

Penelope was glad but wary of the crazy teen.

"Select the car with the CD player. I want to try something on the way back after Colleen's appointment."

"Okay, anything I should know?"

"Colleen might respond to music."

Hugh thought about her comment.

"I don't know except the ice cream did work with Randi."

"Trust me, I think Colleen needs more stimulus in her life. Is this office always so quiet? I expected more excitement."

Hugh was happy her jacket was clean. He laughed. "We are always glad for a slower pace. Don't worry, things will heat up."

GRAY AREA FOR A WOMAN

7 Thursday - Colleen

Penelope waited with Hugh for the coffee machine to stop brewing. He poured the dark coffee into his cup and she did the same.

"Have you seen Liam lately?"

Penelope thought about the last time she saw him.

"Tuesday morning is when he was at his desk."

"I see him now. He's with our boss."

Penelope moved her tall fern and saw the back of Liam's head. She was glad there were no more flowers delivered. She bit her lip.

"Problem?" asked Hugh.

"I didn't read the card on the flowers that arrived Tuesday. That was a mistake. Let me talk to Carter."

Penelope went to Carter's desk, and he was nowhere around. The urn was missing from his desk. She went back to her desk. Carter threw away the urn was her thoughts. The card didn't matter.

"We can go now."

The two walked toward the exit.

Liam saw them leave when he came out of the boss's office. He gathered his things and left. Stepping into his sportscar, Liam drove back to his home. He had been following the case of Duane Hicks and the mysterious other women. Liam needed to rest. Tomorrow was a scheduled interview with a woman who was in jail for trying to steal a different sailboat. He debated about taking Penelope to the interview.

"There's no way she will stay in the vehicle."

Liam would need to include her in the investigation per his boss.

"Duane, you were lucky you didn't take those women to Mexico. We're finding out that they were bad news."

The more Liam thought about the turn of events, Duane knew what the women were up to and bailed out. The man was careful like a cat.

"Where did you bail?"

Meanwhile, Hugh turned into the detention facility parking lot. Penelope watched as he called the front desk.

"We are here to pick up Colleen Brewster. Detective Farris and Detective King are outside in our vehicle."

Penelope waited. The phone rang and Hugh picked up.

"I see. Should we wait? No, of course, we can do this some other day."

Hugh looked at Penelope in disgust.

"Colleen is missing. They think she is somewhere inside the facility. We've been dismissed for today."

"Dismissed? Shouldn't we give her a few more minutes? She might have used the restroom."

Hugh frowned.

"Someone always escorts her to and from the restroom."

Penelope wondered about the comment.

"She can't even go to the restroom. That's strange. This is like a prison."

GRAY AREA FOR A WOMAN

There was a knock at Penelope's window. Standing outside was the missing teen. Penelope rolled her window down.

"Hi, Colleen, are you ready to go to your new appointment? We figured you were in the restroom and needed a minute."

Colleen nodded. Penelope stepped out and opened the back door for her. Colleen settled herself inside. Penelope shut the door. Hugh called the facility and told them they were on their way to the appointment with Colleen.

Penelope smiled when she looked in the mirror at Colleen. The teen seemed calm. Hugh looked over at Penelope. He talked loudly.

"We're on our way. What music is on the CD?"

Penelope rattled off the songs.

"Those songs work. We get to play them on the way back to the teen facility," said Hugh.

After Colleen saw her new person, they drove her back to the detention facility.

On the way back, the music was played. On occasion, Penelope would sing along, and Hugh would hum. Colleen weaved back and forth.

The car came to a stop and two guards came to get Colleen. Both Hugh and Penelope walked with them inside. Hugh talked to the administrator, and Penelope saw Colleen to her room.

"I hope you had a good day. Mr. Farris went to talk to the people at the facility. Hopefully, they will understand you might on occasion want to do things by yourself."

The teen made no conversation. Penelope nodded to the guard that she was ready. Colleen surprised her by talking.

"Bye."

Penelope looked at Colleen and waved. She understood. The teen wanted some things her way. Freedom was difficult in the facility. Colleen was used to being alone living at her mom's place.

"See you next time, I hope."

Hugh met Penelope outside. He was waiting next to their vehicle.

"I've told them she likes music. They will implement some music in her program and let her use the restroom by herself."

"Good. Colleen needs some normalcy in her routine. How about we try the place that makes three-inch Rueben's nine inches long. We can split one. I'll eat the sauerkraut and swiss cheese."

"You're on. The sauerkraut gives me gas."

After lunch, they stopped by Randi's house. His mom was working, and he was shooting baskets with a new ball. Penelope got some of the detectives to chip in for the ball. Hugh played a few games with him.

"How about we try some ice cream?"

"The ice cream is gone," said Randi.

Penelope caught the car keys Hugh threw her. She drove to the small grocery store, purchased some cones, and bought a gallon of chocolate swirl ice cream. Driving back to the house, Randi's mom walked into the yard. Penelope handed her the bag. The two women went inside and fixed the cones.

GRAY AREA FOR A WOMAN

When Hugh and Penelope left, there was a wide smile on Randi and his mother's face. They drove back to headquarters and went to their desks.

Penelope looked up and was surprised to see Hugh at her desk.

"My wife called and wanted to know if we can do this dinner next Thursday. Our son has fallen, and she's at the doctor's office getting stitches in his leg."

"No problem. Next week is fine with me."

Penelope sat at her desk and stared at the screen, waiting for Hugh's report.

Liam sat down in the extra chair.

"Hi, Liam, I thought you left for home."

He sighed and yawned.

"I couldn't sleep. My conscious was bothering me."

He handed her the florist card. She took the note and looked at him questioning how he found the paper.

"I offered to throw the urn away. The envelope flap was open from the water. I read the note and thought you might have missed the card."

Liam stood up and walked away.

Penelope opened the tiny envelope and read the note.

Loved the silver dress. Dinner, my place? ME.

She blushed that her boss read the note. Penelope knew she would need to respond. She stuffed the note in her bag.

Penelope drove home. Walking to her apartment, she noticed her door was partially open. Unbuckling her gun, she slowly opened her door and looked around. Nothing seemed disturbed except there was a glass ashtray on the counter with a cigarette butt. The butt didn't contain lipstick.

Immediately, she called her apartment security people. The man came and gave her a piece of letterhead paper. Penelope read the contents.

"The leasing people went through my apartment today to do their check on the tenants. Where is my sixty-day required notice per my lease agreement?"

The man told her the leasing people thought they smelled gas.

"They called the gas company."

"The smell was a false alarm."

Penelope watched as the security man went away. She called her father who told her to turn in her notice to cancel the lease. Tomorrow she should go to the condominium building four blocks further north. Warren gave her the address and phone number.

"What about a down payment? I have about five thousand dollars toward a purchase."

Her father told her they would work out a payback plan. She was to buy the biggest unit. He wanted her out of this apartment building. She also wanted out. Penelope locked her apartment and drove to a hotel. She called Marvin to let him know she was busy this weekend and possibly the next.

Penelope ate dinner in the hotel restaurant and went to bed. Suddenly, she awoke.

"I forgot about my clothes."

She remembered the hotel held a small boutique shop. There were some exercise clothes and spa robes. Finding the card to the boutique, the shop opened at seven in the morning.

"There should be enough time to buy something and get to work."

Penelope couldn't believe her bad luck with the apartment.

"Better to bale now."

8 Friday – Interview with Madeline

Liam was impressed to see Penelope in a hot pink velour sweat outfit when he stopped by her desk.

A small flowerpot of pink striped petunias sat on her desk with a card and a bottle of pink rose wine. His eyes looked down, and he tried to figure what might be on the small card that lay turned over.

"Nice outfit. The new casual look caught me off guard. No one wears hot pink in this office that I can recall, but I've only been here for ten years."

"I'm moving. Hot pink rotates every five years per my mom."

Liam could now understand the outfit.

"Didn't you just get here? Your apartment somehow is a problem."

"The leasing people entered my apartment without authorization. They gave me a bogus letter dated after they went into my apartment. I called the gas company. The apartment people lied to me. There was no call to them about a gas leak. Therefore, I stayed in a hotel last night. I'm going to have to leave at two today to check out a condominium for sale. My dad agrees with me."

Liam pondered her problem.

"We can quit early. I'll go with you. I can help make sure the new building is safe."

"That's not necessary. The building is brand new. My parents have already checked the place out when they were here. They were thinking of buying a place in LA. I'll look for a two to three-bedroom now.

My dad likes the larger unit. We're going to purchase the property together."

"What about moving your things?"

"I've already covered the boxes. The storage company put them aside. I don't have much to pack. No furniture or heavy stuff."

"Hey, I'm good with boxes."

Penelope stuffed the flower card in her bag.

"I'll let you know. I'm ready for some appointments that we have scheduled for today. The destination shows the place is jail. There is a female incarcerated, and I didn't see a name listed on my sheet printout. Who is she?"

Liam knew she was ready to go to work.

"Right this way. We'll take my car today. The person is Madeline Foster, and she is awaiting trial for stolen property."

They approached Liam's sports car and she sat in the front seat. Buckling her seatbelt, she waited until they were on the freeway.

"Your car is impressive. What did she steal?"

Liam knew his partner would be interested.

"A forty-five-foot sailboat loaded with the best kind of gear possible. Radios, radar, a large motor, huge sails, and an expensive life raft in case the sails don't fill out. This boat is a dream come true. She stole the luxury boat from some idiot bloke who trusted her."

"This sailboat wasn't moored in Ventura by any chance?"

"You are a lucky guesser," mentioned Liam.

"This Madeline person was going to steal Duane Hicks's sailboat originally. Instead, she found a better luxury boat."

Liam chuckled.

"The owner has a huge loan on the boat. He looked rich. Immediately, the police were notified. She found out too late. The bank hired a top firm to diligently locate the boat. The bank's connections to expert resources put her in a pickle. The police were notified, found her and the boat in a quiet cove, and quickly made the arrest. We hope she likes to talk. We could use the information for our case. Ms. Madeline Foster might be the last person to talk with Duane."

"Duane didn't want to take the ladies to Mexico. He smelled trouble," said Penelope.

"Our thoughts exactly."

"How did you find this woman or know of her existence?"

Liam changed lanes.

"People talk, and Hugh mentioned boaters like to party and take pictures. I followed through. Madeline's name popped up in the system from a picture a boater gave me. She has been arrested before her unlucky adventure into a cove."

They pulled into the county jail parking garage and went inside. The guards brought the handcuffed woman to their room. Penelope recognized the green and white suits assigned to the jail tenants.

"Ms. Foster, we are Los Angeles detectives investigating another case regarding a missing person. We thought maybe you could help us. You knew Duane

Hicks, and we would like to know if you have any idea where he might have gone?"

Madeline's eyes darted back and forth between the two detectives.

"I shouldn't talk to you without my lawyer. He told me to watch out for any smart detectives who like to confuse people."

"We won't ask you any questions regarding your current case."

He tossed a picture toward her. She looked at Duane Hicks's picture.

"I don't know him."

Liam slid a second photo across of Madeline talking with Duane on a boat dock in Ventura. The outside barbeque restaurant was in the background.

"I might have talked with this man, but I don't remember our conversation."

Liam rubbed his face and slid a picture of Mason Jarett.

"Mr. Jarett remembers you sitting at the barbeque restaurant outdoors last year with three other women. Therefore, we figure you might have talked to both Mason and Duane about sailing. You like boats."

"Okay, I did talk with both men about sailing around the area and south to San Diego. We talked about the technical gear required to sail these waters. I was curious. Talking is not a crime. They appeared friendly. I'm a friendly girl. I grew up around Ventura and like the boat people. Sometimes I get a free dinner and go to their parties."

Liam looked at Penelope and nodded.

"Did you ever have dinner with Duane?" asked Penelope.

She rubbed her hair and the cuffs clanked.

"I hate this metal."

Madeline made a face at the guard.

"Once or twice, we might have eaten dinner. Duane didn't have any food on his boat. He volunteered to give me a ride to Mexico."

"And did he offer a ride to your three friends?"

Madeline looked at Penelope.

"He did except he wanted to meet them."

Liam sat up in his chair. He now knew the other three women existed. As of this morning, the police had no names for Madeline's accomplices in her current crime.

"Did Duane meet them in Ventura?"

The young woman sighed.

"Just once and not all of them."

Penelope asked the next logical question.

"You don't know where Duane went?"

The prisoner shook her head.

"We would like to ask the other three girls if Duane mentioned someplace that he wanted to visit in the future. Your friends might be able to help us."

"I told you not all the girls met this Duane guy. We were only acquaintances. Besides, the girls are gone. As soon as I was arrested, they were splits-villa. In other words, I'm on my own for the bigger sailboat charge."

Liam took over.

"If you could give us their names, we might be able to ask them. If you talked to the girls about Duane, they might have been curious and saw him later. It doesn't hurt for us to ask."

He handed her a piece of paper and an ink pen.

Madeline took her time. She passed the written names to Liam.

"My pen?"

Madeline took her clenched hand and opened it to reveal the pen. Liam took the pen. He read the names.

"Beth, Connie, and Deann."

"Dee Anne liked Duane. He liked her back. It was the only time she met him that I'm aware of. I never knew their last names."

"How about an address of where they lived?"

The woman tried to think.

"Some rentals around Pomona. Connie lived with this guy named Cougar."

"Thank you for your help, Madeline. If we find Duane, I'll put in a good word to your attorney who will know how to benefit you," said Liam.

He nodded to the guard who took Ms. Foster back to jail.

Liam called the police to investigate the man named Cougar, and he gave them the first names of the three accomplices.

They drove back to headquarters. Liam turned off his car.

"We may have helped the other case. Ours is at a standstill until we can talk with this Deann. She might have made a connection with Duane. She might also know the last names of the others. But we don't know her full name. Where are you staying tonight?"

Penelope didn't want to return to her old apartment, but she needed clothes.

"I'll go back to my old apartment."

"Why don't I go with you to view the condominiums? I can take my car."

Penelope thought about the meeting with the condominium manager.

"All right."

She dug out the brochure with the address and gave it to him.

"Meet you in the lobby."

9 New Condominium

Penelope and Liam met the condominium manager and looked at three units. She called her father and talked with him while Liam looked at the fitness center with the manager.

"Good equipment and the setup are a great use of space."

Penelope, her father, and her mother chose the three-bedroom corner condominium. She put a deposit down and scanned the documents to her father's attorney for review.

After her business was finished with the manager, she and Liam returned to their vehicles.

"This is a nice complex. Their security and amenities are top-notch. Your parents will have more room when they visit."

"I should get back to my apartment and start packing."

"Tell you what? Let's pick up a hot pizza for dinner. I can bring your boxes tomorrow morning and help pack."

Penelope was hungry.

"Is there some reason you are being overly nice to me today?"

Liam leaned on his car door.

"I don't know. I think I'm still trying to make amends for taking your flower card. Plus, the jail interview went well."

"There's a pizza place a couple of blocks from my apartment. We can leave our cars at the apartment and walk."

The two detectives drove back and walked to the pizza place. There were so many people, they ordered their pizza to go. On her apartment patio, they ate and drank beer.

They went back inside. Penelope was putting the leftover pizza in the refrigerator when there was a knock on her door. Liam went to answer the door. Standing there was the apartment security guard.

"We've encountered a person on the third floor who tried to break into one of the apartments. The police recommended that we notify the rest of the tenants."

"Did they catch the person?" asked Liam.

"No, he got away."

"Great! Goodnight."

Liam shut the door and watched the expression on Penelope's face. She appeared rattled.

"Why don't I stay overnight on the couch, and we can get the boxes in the morning?"

"I can handle things."

Liam hesitated.

"I know you can except there is a problem. I'll worry about you being here alone."

Penelope went to her closet and brought out a blanket and an extra pillow.

"Thank you."

She went back to her bedroom and closed the door. Liam was going to text Becka and thought better of it. He hadn't planned anything with his girlfriend for tonight. He was free to stay. Liam placed a chair in front of the apartment door.

"At least I'll hear the creep coming inside."

In the morning Liam picked up the reserved boxes, packing paper, and tape. He returned with bagels and cream cheese for breakfast. They finished packing her boxes. The time was around eleven.

"I don't think you should stay here tonight."

Penelope opened the leftover pizza box, and they ate cold pizza.

"I'll stay in a hotel room. They said I could move into the condominium on Wednesday morning."

Liam thought fast.

"Four nights in a hotel will be expensive. We could load your boxes in both our cars and take them to my place for safekeeping. My laundry room is large enough to accommodate the boxes. I do have a perfectly safe guest room which you may use rather than pay two to three hundred dollars a night in a hotel room. Plus, there's my freezer full of meat."

Penelope thought about her predicament. Liam was the lesser of two evils.

"What about Becka? She wouldn't understand. There's also my parents and people at work."

Liam could take care of Becka.

"No need to worry. I'm not telling your father nor anyone at the office."

"I don't know."

Liam picked up two boxes and left the apartment. Penelope frowned.

"I guess the decision has been made."

When Liam returned, she handed him two more boxes.

"They do have a cart in the lobby."

"I was trying to impress you with my muscles. Next trip, I'll bring the cart. Then you can turn in your apartment keys and we can be gone."

"Wait."

Liam turned around.

"I don't know where you live?"

Liam smiled.

"I have a house close to the beach."

Penelope stood with pen and paper in hand. He told her the address.

"Wonderful beach area," said Penelope.

"Only the best will do."

10 Liam's House by the Beach

Penelope pulled into the small driveway. Liam stood in the garage doorway. His car was neatly tucked inside and empty of boxes. He helped carry the rest of the boxes into the laundry room. She locked her car and went inside his home.

Liam showed her where to store her suitcase and toiletries. Next, he took her on a tour of his home. The large master bedroom, closet, bath, exercise room, and office were upstairs. The guest bedroom, main bath, kitchen, and living room were on the first floor. The kitchen and rest of the place looked newly renovated.

"I like your home. The rooms are friendly."

She looked in the refrigerator and was surprised how well stocked it was with food. There were a couple of bags of lettuce and bottles of good dressing. At least she could eat.

"Now would be a good time to walk to the beach. I'll grab us some water."

They walked and jogged together until they reached the water's edge. The waves touched their tennis shoes.

"I usually jog for a mile north and turn around. The breakwater gets dangerous at high tide. You can jog south for about another mile. Don't jog at night. The bums come out."

She nodded.

"I want to let you know that I appreciate the invitation. For a minute there when the guard told us about the break-in, I had a panic moment which must seem strange to you. A detective with a gun worried about a burglar might seem odd."

Liam reached for her hand.

"Even cops and detectives have moments. You shouldn't worry about my reaction. You are in a job most women avoid. Call our job titles a very gray area for females. You have to work harder to control your instinct to run."

He let go of her hand.

"We should head back. I have some work to do this evening. I took out steaks for dinner. There's a small grill on the porch outside the kitchen."

"Good. I can make a salad."

He laughed because the lettuce was in bags.

"You can help peel the potatoes. I like to make my fresh potato fries on the grill."

They returned to his home. Penelope went to the guest room to unpack. She took her computer out and read the note and documents from her parents. All the real estate documents were signed and accepted by the condominium. She squealed with delight. She would have her new place and could move into the condominium on Wednesday morning.

She called her father. Penelope told them she was packed and moved out. She was safely at a coworker's place. They didn't ask for a person's name, and she didn't offer one.

Penelope went into the kitchen and looked for an iron. She gave up and threw her two blouses in the dryer with a wet washcloth. After twenty minutes, she took them out and hung them up. Tomorrow she would pick up her other suit and blouses from the cleaners.

Liam returned to the kitchen.

"You are settled in the guest room"

"Yes, the guest room looks comfortable. I will own the condominium and can move on Wednesday morning. I thought you could put some of the boxes in your car. I could make two trips from the office, so you don't need to take time off."

"Great job on purchasing the condo. If you need anything while you are here, let me know."

Liam handed her a key to the front door. She put the key in her room.

They peeled potatoes and readied the grill.

Liam was pleased she was in his home. He told Becka he was busy on a difficult case and couldn't see her until Thursday evening. He didn't realize his nosy neighbor saw Penelope when they were outside grilling.

In the morning, Liam made them coffee and an egg sandwich. They drove separately to work as if nothing strange happened over the weekend.

11 Third Week – Who's Cougar

Penelope went to her desk and saw the dried plant. She forgot about the pink striped petunias. When she tried to move the pot, dried leaves fell onto her desk. She dumped the dead thing into her garbage can and was sweeping the dried leaves into the garbage when Liam appeared.

There was a strange smirk on his face.

"Quiet. I forgot about the plant. My mother is better with plants than I am."

"Let me understand. You don't cook, clean the house, or take care of plants. Let's not mention that I showed you how to peel potatoes. Mental note filed away. Penelope is an innocent bystander to the workings of everyday living."

She hit him in the arm.

"I didn't print the work schedule. Where are we going today?"

Liam moved out of Penelope's way and followed her to the garage. He signed for a vehicle, and they drove out of the lot.

"Dugan has some information for me regarding Cougar. I called him Saturday while we were moving your boxes."

Penelope remained silent.

"The egg sandwich was good. You must have a thing-a-ma-jig that keeps the egg round while frying."

"I do have special tools in my kitchen. They are in the righthand drawer. Any other questions about the house?"

GRAY AREA FOR A WOMAN

"When did you get your coffee machine?"

Now Liam laughed.

"Two days after I saw your machine at the office. I liked the coffee. Here we are at the supper club. I suppose you won't stay in the car?"

Penelope opened her door and stepped out. She let him lead the way. A man was standing outside, and he let them enter. Her eyes quickly adjusted to the dark. Liam was already sitting at the bar. She sat down on a stool with two stools between them.

Dugan looked at Liam.

"You need to stop visiting me so much. My neighbors have complained."

Dugan handed over a cup of coffee to Liam and a charged water to Penelope. Liam took a sip.

"New brand?"

"Antiqua," said Dugan.

Liam waited.

"Perhaps Ms. King could check out the stage. We need to talk in private."

Penelope went over to the piano and sat down at the keyboard. She played a little bit of music and stopped. Liam was in some heated argument with Dugan. The two men stopped talking.

Penelope walked back to the bar.

"Your piano needs tuning."

Dugan looked at her as if he had no idea what she was talking about.

"She's correct," said Liam.

Dugan yelled and a man approached.

"Get the piano fixed."

Dugan slid a piece of paper to Liam. Liam opened the note and read the man's name.

"I owe you two favors."

Dugan looked at Penelope and back at Liam. Liam stared at Dugan without blinking. There was no way Dugan was getting a date with his partner.

Dugan backed down from the stare. Penelope wasn't sure what passed between the men.

"Detective King, we have to talk to a second snitch. The man is a lifeguard."

Penelope followed Liam to the car. He drove toward the beach and pulled into the lot. They went toward the lifeguard tower. One of the lifeguards talked with Liam. Penelope watched the boys with their surfboards. Two of the boys were doing things wrong. She walked over to them and talked.

Liam saw her and joined the group. She was showing them how to hold their bodies for proper balance.

"Detective King, we need to move along," said Liam. They walked back to the car and sat.

"You know how to surf. I never learned. Someday I might take a lesson."

"Sure, surfing is popular here and lots of other places. You have information regarding the case?"

"Cougar does have a name. Syd Coogan is the man we need to talk with regarding the three women. I've texted the name to the police. We'll wait to see what they find. The lifeguard knew Cougar's girlfriend. They used to room together three years ago. He mentioned she was getting stranger, and that's why they parted. The girlfriend is Connie Moore."

GRAY AREA FOR A WOMAN

Penelope watched the waves.

"Connie is one of the three women we are trying to find."

Liam handed her a mint he picked up from Dugan's place. She unwrapped the mint and put it in her mouth.

"The police are running her name as well."

She looked at Liam.

"You talked with our Captain this morning and seemed a little off after your meeting."

Liam thought about telling her. He would be in Greece next week when the man would be released.

"Donnie Corwin gets out next Wednesday. I'll be in Greece. I did let Dugan know."

Penelope shook her head.

"Why would Dugan care?"

"Dugan helped us find Donnie the first time. He was upset the police let him out. He blamed me. Hence, all the heated discussion and shouting this morning."

Liam's phone rang. She watched as he listened. After ten minutes, he hung up.

"We're going back to the office. Some case files will be coming across."

They returned and both read Cougar's rap sheet. Reading Connie's past was the worst.

"I'm going home. There's some chicken, vegetables, and skewers waiting."

Penelope waited a respectable time before she also left. When she reached Liam's house, she went to change. Picking a white terrycloth short and matching short sleeve hoodie, she went into the kitchen where Liam was staring into space. He looked at her outfit.

"Nice legs."

"Oh, I should probably change again. I grabbed the most comfortable thing out of my suitcase."

"Hey, I'm cool with seeing sexy legs. You looked different is all. Business suits hide warm bodies."

He was talking too much.

"I'll get the kebobs ready for the oven."

She watched as he wrapped them in foil and put them in the hot oven. He set the timer for twenty minutes. He set the plates, silverware, and napkins on the bar.

"I should help. Why use foil?"

"Please sit. The foil keeps the oven cleaner. Any leftovers can be tossed in the freezer. Putting them in foil saves time. It's been nice having company in the evenings."

Penelope thought so, too. She made her offer.

"Why don't I buy us some dinner tomorrow? We can go to the wharf before we come home."

"I'd like to have dinner out. There are good restaurants around the piers."

The timer buzzed. She helped unwrap a kebob and removed the metal skewer.

"Ouch, the wire is hot."

Liam looked at her finger. He took a clean dishrag and put an ice cube inside.

"Here, put this on your finger. I'll undo the rest of the kebobs."

She watched as he undid a kebob on her plate. She held up her hand. One kebob was enough. Using her fork, she cut the chicken, pineapple, mushroom, and green peppers. Penelope liked the flavor.

"Lemon pepper is the secret ingredient on the kebob."

"Liam, the Connie person has got a long rap sheet since age fifteen. Larceny, stealing cars, drugs, possible attempted murder, child endangerment, etc."

"She's one sweet broad. There is no love inside."

"You think Cougar is along for the ride?"

Liam helped himself to a second kebob.

"I do, but I don't think he will rat his girlfriend out."

"Too afraid of what she will do?"

Liam handed her the mushroom with his fork. She took the large bite.

"Yep. I think he should be afraid. The attempted murder charge couldn't be proven. Although the idea of brake failure at the correct moment appears odd, not to mention the one-hundred-foot cliff. The guy that died was a past boyfriend."

Penelope put down her fork.

"Connie Moore has a bad temper."

Liam removed her plate to the sink. The uneaten kebobs were placed in the freezer. He dug out ice cream sandwiches from the refrigerator.

"Not me, but I'll put the dishes in the dishwasher."

He watched her tidy up the kitchen. His phone vibrated. Liam saw Becka's name on the screen.

"I've got to take a private call."

Penelope finished loading the dishwasher, found the soap, and started the machine. She wiped the center island, made sure the stove was turned off and hung up the dishcloth. Her finger looked better.

She looked in the living room and realized Liam went outside the front. She sat down and flipped through the newspaper. After fifteen minutes, she gave up and went to her room.

Penelope was lying on the bed. It was nine-thirty, and she was tired. She read her email. There was a note from the condominium people regarding parking, and pickup of her keys. She was excited there was only a day and a half to wait. She would have her place.

"Furniture might be a little bit of a problem arriving Wednesday afternoon."

Her bed, a couch, and two loungers were scheduled for delivery. The rugs and rest of the furniture were three or four weeks out.

Liam knocked on her door.

"Come in."

"Sorry about the call. I wanted to make sure you were tucked in for the evening."

"I'm fine. I will see you in the morning."

"Goodnight, Penelope."

She looked at the clock. The time was ten-thirty. She turned out her light and fell soundly asleep. Penelope felt safe.

12 Tuesday Evening & Kung Pau

After her day with Hugh, she waited for Liam in the office. They agreed to meet at five o'clock for their dinner at the wharf. A strange woman was sitting on Liam's desk. Hugh came bustling around the corner and sat down with a thump in her extra chair.

"Now tell me about your new condominium. I know the address from their website. The place looks gorgeous. The kids and wife want to try the beach someday when the weather is hot."

Penelope's eyes lit up.

"Of course, you can come for a visit. We can picnic on the beach. Cold meat and veggie wraps would be fun. Fruit kebobs and potato chips in baggies seem appropriate. The kids could help make and assemble them. Who's the woman on Liam's desk?"

Hugh looked sheepish.

"Liam called me. He asked that I let you know there's been a change of plans."

"Becka is the change?"

Hugh wrung his hands together.

"He didn't exactly explain other than the two of you were scheduled to go to the wharf. I don't know why you were going to the wharf. You could be discussing your Cougar case or something."

Penelope trusted Hugh. She decided to confide in him.

"My apartment was having burglar break-in issues and unscheduled security checks. Therefore, I decided to leave Saturday. The condominium wasn't available until tomorrow. I needed a place to stay. Liam offered. Tonight, was payback like in dinner as a thank you to a colleague."

Hugh's eyes bulged in shock.

"You stayed at Liam's house!"

Penelope looked at Hugh.

"There is nothing to worry about. We were fine. He was the perfect host. We cooked together. I burned my finger on the kebob metal. The guest room bed was comfortable. However, don't go telling anyone in the office. They might get the wrong idea."

Hugh nodded.

"Absolutely the wrong idea. I'm seeing the whole picture."

Now Penelope was upset. She hissed, "We were perfectly normal adults."

"Sure, you were normal. Liam is far from normal. This is terrible. What if Becka finds out? She'll assume the worst."

"I'm not going to tell her, and neither are you."

Hugh rubbed his lip. He looked at her doubtfully.

"I thought you were seeing the District Attorney."

Penelope looked horrified.

"Where did you get that idea?"

"You know, the flowers and the Andersen party in a sexy dress."

Penelope shook her head.

"You are close. My dress was like the other ladies' dresses at the party. My mom said to do elegant. I wore the elegant. Marvin would like more. But he's

83

older and getting divorced which are big issues with me. There's too much conflict."

Hugh thought about her words.

"Marvin's rich, not bad looking, and has a great big house *on the beach*, in Malibu, no less. Are you crazy? Women would kill to date him. I still think your dress was sexy, and I'm married."

"Marvin's already asked me to come to Malibu."

Hugh perked up.

"The next time he asks, you should go. Test the water. You are single. He's almost single."

Penelope leaned around Hugh.

"Becka is gone. I can go back to Liam's house."

Hugh watched her leave. He went to his desk and shoved some papers in his briefcase. Liam approached.

"Where's Penelope?"

Hugh shook his head.

"I gave her your message. She went back to your house."

Liam stopped in his tracks.

"She told you?"

"I'm going home to my lovely wife and hyperactive kids. The place is always chaos, but I'm happy. Underscore happy part. Happily married to my live-in wife. We sleep together in the same bed. Are you insane! She's dating the DA."

"No, she's not. Penelope would have told me."

"What? You are best friends after she sleeps at your house? I heard about the kebobs. Trust me, she wants to go to Marvin's house in Malibu. She's thinking about it."

Hugh pulled the zipper on his briefcase and left.

Liam sat on Hugh's desk.

"This has been insane. What's with the house in Malibu? A different beach is all."

He ordered Chinese takeout and drove home. Penelope's car wasn't in his driveway. He was going to call her when his garage door opened. Her car was in the garage.

"Hi, I thought our dinner plans changed."

Liam handed her the take-out bags.

"This smells good."

They went into his house. He punched the button to the garage door.

For now, they were safe. He didn't dare ask her about the District Attorney. All the flowers from him went into the trash.

"Hugh is wrong. I've got to hold things together one more day," said Liam to himself. He knew Becka was getting tired of his excuses.

He brightened as he saw his partner's face light up.

"I love Kung Pao chicken! How did you know?" asked Penelope.

The sesame chicken was her order. Liam quickly recovered.

"We can share this evening?"

Liam grabbed an expensive bottle of wine from the wine refrigerator under the island. Penelope grabbed the glasses out of the cupboard. He poured the yellow liquid.

GRAY AREA FOR A WOMAN

"To your new condominium!"

They clinked glasses and dug into the cardboard cartons.

Penelope's face was flushed with pleasure.

13 Wednesday – Furniture Arrival

Penelope took the new sheet sets out of their box and made her bed. She was glad to have a bed frame and expensive mattresses. She threw the white blanket over the sheet and placed the pillows on top. Then she laid down.

"This is heaven."

Her phone rang. The call was from Liam.

"How are things going in your newly-purchased condominium?"

"I have a bed, a couch, and two chairs."

"Well, at least you have the important stuff."

Liam wondered if she was wearing the short terry cloth outfit.

She sat up and went into the living room. There were some frozen dinner or sandwiches in the refrigerator for supper.

"The reason for my call is to remind you. This Friday, you will be with Hugh. I'm off to Greece."

Penelope remembered he was leaving.

"When will you return to Los Angeles?"

He chuckled.

"Why do you want to know?"

"As a thank you, I owe you at least one or two surfing lessons since we didn't do dinner. You saved me hotel fees. My father is sending me my surfboard."

Liam saw Becka's car in the driveway.

"We'll talk about lessons when I return."

"Great."

They both disconnected from the call.

GRAY AREA FOR A WOMAN

She called her parents and then microwaved a meal.

"This is close to cooking."

She looked for a hot pad. There weren't any. She grabbed the kitchen towel.

Hugh called to make sure they were on for dinner on Thursday night. None of his children showed any illness, and he forbid them from riding their bikes. So, there would be no stitches. She assured him she was ready for a chaotic dinner on Thursday. Real food sounded wonderful.

"Do you have hot pads? I could get you some new ones."

She tossed the half-eaten meal. The picture on the box always looked delicious. Penelope sent herself a note to buy hot pads. Hugh told her about a great grilling shop on the way to his house.

Satisfied there were no more calls to make, she unpacked her boxes and went to bed.

In the morning she went to work. There were a dozen red roses in a crystal vase on her desk. The crystal was expensive. Quickly opening the card, she read the note.

"Marvin thinks he has won the Malibu house and wants me to swim with him this Saturday as a celebration. Test the water. What if I drown? Not to worry, you can swim. How big is a pool anyway?"

Penelope tapped the card as she debated. She looked at her phone and dialed Marvin's number on the card.

LINDA MCKOWN

When Liam arrived at the office at ten o'clock, most of the detectives were out of the office. He was waiting for Captain Harrison. They had a meeting.

Liam walked over to Penelope's desk and saw the extravagant bouquet. The card was missing.

"Mental note, the woman likes big roses and expensive crystal."

For some reason, the bouquet put him in a bad mood. He walked over to Hugh's desk and looked at his paper calendar.

"Dinner with Penelope. At least she will have fun this evening and a hearty meal."

He saw his boss arrived. Liam grabbed his computer bag with the necessary files and went into his boss's office. After two hours, Liam left to go home to pack.

Once home, he jogged to the beach. He wasn't sure this was a good time to fly off to a foreign country. There were too many things happening on his open cases. He threw a shell at a seagull. The bird squawked and flew off.

A person sat down next to him.

"I thought I would find you here. What's wrong?"

He looked at Becka.

"I don't know. There's an edgy feeling happening."

She watched the large seagull approach and look at Liam.

"We could cancel."

Liam felt trapped.

"No, your family is waiting for our arrival. We fly to Greece as planned."

She snuggled closer.

"Good. For a minute there, I thought that we lost each other. You need to get away from work I hardly get to see you."

He dusted the sand off his hands and stood. He pulled her up.

"You are probably right."

Liam walked away from her. Becka knew her friend had a bad week. He hadn't kissed her today. She followed him to his house. She was pleased they were leaving incredibly early in the morning.

The seagull flew away.

14 First Dinner at Hugh's

Hugh opened wide his door. Three children burst forth and hugged her legs. Penelope couldn't move. Hugh gave a command, and they let go.

"Sorry. They have eaten and get to meet you before going to bed. I should have warned you they like to hug. I believe they are in a phase until age nine. At nine, no more bear hugs."

"You are wrong, kids quit hugs around twelve, but I forgive you."

Penelope entered the foyer and was introduced to his children and wife. A maid ushered the children upstairs and off to bed. She handed him the bag of new hot pads and a bottle of wine.

"We have a friend of ours help us whenever we have guests. Emma insists she can't cook and deal with the whole family scene. Come into the dining room. Dinner will be on time and be exceptionally good. These hot pads are the best. They have super-insulating power. Do you mind if we skip the wine? The kids made punch."

"I like to drink punch."

Hugh needed to tell her.

"They dropped the jar in the punchbowl. All the maraschino cherries and juice fell out. Emma retrieved the cherries and froze them."

Penelope knew the punch was over-sweetened.

"My mom liked lemons."

Hugh was relieved.

"Emma, add a few lemons."

GRAY AREA FOR A WOMAN

Penelope was pleased to see good china and elegant covered dishes on the table with tapered candles. Hugh lit the candles, and his wife brought a huge platter of roast with slices of cooked squash and fresh basil. She was pleased to see cooked noodles with asparagus in cream sauce. The glasses of punch were poured.

They sat down and ate. Hugh encouraged her to take more. She took a second piece of squash. The maid person returned and helped remove the dishes. A cold vanilla pudding was for dessert.

They went into the living room and drank steaming coffee.

Hugh's wife, Emma, sat down next to her.

"How do you like LA? This must be different from Billings and New York City."

"First, I want to thank you for a wonderful dinner. Last night my meal was a terrible frozen fish weird thing which was not recognizable. The company was from Iowa. Are there lakes there?"

Emma squeezed Penelope's arm.

"I have no idea. We try to have a large meal on Thursday evening because we can have leftovers Friday. Weekends are pizza and hamburgers or anything on the grill. Hugh takes over. Our kids try to help."

"I like that you keep the structure. The answers to your question. I like Montana and New York but love the warmer climate. There's not much surfing in either of the last two places."

Hugh piped up, "I didn't know you surf."

"The exercise is better than a gym any day. I might get to teach Liam when he returns, and the weather gets warmer."

Emma raised her eyebrows.

"I forgot that you also are partnering with Liam. We should have invited him to tonight's dinner."

Emma gave an evil look at her husband.

"I told you Liam is leaving early tomorrow for Greece."

"Ah, yes, I do remember. Becka has family there. They own a villa in Corinth."

There was a quiet period while they drank their coffee.

"I miss Liam. He is great fun and remarkably interesting," commented Emma.

Penelope swallowed.

"His home is nice. I liked to jog to the beach when I was there this past week."

Emma picked up immediately on the words.

"Liam invited you to his home. How lovely? His home is the right size for a bachelor. I've seen the guest room. The room looked comfortable."

Hugh needed to intervene.

"Penelope also knows the DA."

Emma turned.

"How do you know Marvin Edmond?"

"My parents know him. They met while at a golf tournament in LA. Plus, we went to Andersen's party together."

Emma looked at her husband.

"I'm sorry I missed their party. I should have gone."

GRAY AREA FOR A WOMAN

Penelope finished her coffee, and Hugh offered her more.

"No thank you but I do need to use the restroom before I leave."

Hugh showed her the entryway bathroom. Penelope picked a plastic duck out of the sink before she washed her hands. She handed Hugh the duck.

"Thank you again. Goodnight."

Hugh walked her to her car. She turned.

"I did accept Marvin's invitation for a swim in his Malibu pool Saturday."

Hugh smiled. There was no way he was going to tell his wife. His wife would tell Liam. Right now, he was rooting for the DA.

"See you tomorrow Penelope. Fridays can't come too soon."

15 Pool Date

Marvin greeted Penelope on Saturday at eleven in the morning.

"Come inside my home. I'm so glad you could make the drive, and you have your swimsuit on under your clothes."

She stepped into his modern white kitchen.

"We have gourmet sandwiches for lunch. I hope you like Philly Steak sandwiches. Let me show you the house."

After the tour, he pointed to the first-floor bathroom. She stepped out of her clothes and stuffed them into her beach bag. Walking out to the back patio and pool, she put her car keys in her bag and stepped out of her sandals. She noted the size of the pool.

"The pool doesn't look too deep. This size is swimmable."

The large white beach towels were in a cabana. She walked over and grabbed three towels. Penelope dropped them near the steps and waited for Marvin. He came out in his red swim trunks with a red hat and expensive sunglasses.

Marvin was talking to someone on the cell phone. Penelope worried her yellow bikini swimsuit was too revealing. There wasn't time to purchase a different suit. This one was a little faded from surfing. The fringe in front was all wrong.

"I look like a hooker."

Marvin watched as she stepped into the pool and started swimming. He threw down his phone and joined her. He swam close and she stopped. She could touch the floor.

"Hi, beautiful. We are finally alone together. I've waited for this moment. I dreamed of being with you under palm trees. Huge palm trees with twinkle lights."

Marvin took her in his arms and kissed her. Penelope hadn't kissed someone for a long time. He kept kissing her.

"Whoa, we have all day. Let's go slow."

Marvin smiled.

"We do have all day. I've dismissed my people. The house is ours. I forgot to turn on the music. I'll be a minute. The clicker is on the kitchen counter."

Marvin let her go.

"Hold your thoughts. I will be back."

Penelope splashed him. He came back to her and grabbed her.

Kissing her once again with more passion, they heard a woman's voice.

"If Romeo would get out of the pool, we can get this discussion over."

Penelope looked at the woman in a designer sundress and heels.

"Oh, no, I thought you turned in your house keys. You told my lawyer that you lost the second set."

"I lied. There was another set somewhere in my other bags."

Marvin turned to Penelope.

"My wife, soon-to-be-ex-wife, has arrived unannounced. She wants something again. This shouldn't take long."

Penelope exited the pool and grabbed a towel while Marvin's wife watched her. She felt extremely self-conscious.

She talked to herself, "Next time, I buy a one-piece swimsuit with no fringe for a pool party for two. Where's my mother when I need her. She goes to the malls and knows which store carries a basic suit."

Marvin went into the house with the strange woman. Penelope could hear them arguing. She looked at the palm trees and could see where the wired lights were wrapped around the trees.

"I bet the trees look pretty at night. Too bad I won't be here. This whole scene is wrong. I should leave."

After drying herself she checked her phone. After ten minutes she put her clothes back on and her sandals. After ten more minutes, Penelope found her car keys and went to her sports car. She started the engine and drove for a way down Highway 1 before turning around.

She pulled over next to a sandwich shop. Her phone hadn't rung. She went into the shop and ordered a tuna croissant sandwich and cola. Unwrapping the sandwich, she drove home while eating.

After an hour at her home, she finally received a text from Marvin asking where she went. She texted back. Penelope turned her phone off and changed her clothes.

Heading in the direction of the shopping center, she bought new towels and a bedspread. A one-piece swimsuit was added to her shopping bags. On a whim, she bought a white bikini. Feeling better, she bought some casual wrap clothes for lounging inside or on the beach.

She went home and washed her hair. Turning on her phone, she deleted Marvin's texts. There was one text from Hugh.

"Having fun yet?"

She texted him back.

"The date was a bust. The wife appeared with her own set of keys."

Hugh texted back.

"Slob. He should have changed the locks."

Penelope agreed.

She was relieved that the date went sour. She wasn't ready for an affair with a detective or a DA.

There was a knock at her door. A delivery man was standing outside with a large box. She signed for the package. Taking a knife, she slowly slit and opened the cardboard. The foam packing was removed.

Inside was an expensive lamp with a glass tray. Penelope put the lamp next to one of the loungers and plugged the cord in the wall. The lampshade was placed on the wire. She clicked the turn-on button and stood back.

"The lamp fits."

Reading the note, she knew her parents were going to fill the condominium at a high rate of speed. There was another box delivered later. It was a large ottoman with sturdy white leather and brass tacks.

"Now all we need is fancy candlesticks made out of antlers."

On Sunday, another box was delivered. She couldn't help but call her parents.

"Where am I supposed to put this antler bowl?"

Her mother told her they were to go into their room. The antler candlesticks were scheduled to arrive Monday with her surfboard. Their condominium manager assured them the packages would be stored in the office for her until she was home from work.

"My life is back to normal."

She looked in her refrigerator.

"I forgot to buy food. Oh, well, tomorrow will be soon enough."

She opened her bedspread and placed the fabric on the bed.

"This is better."

The tags were ripped off the towels and she washed them in the built-in washer. Later the towels were dried and hung up in the bathroom.

A few candles were placed in the bathroom with new soaps.

Penelope walked down to the lobby and out the door. She sat near the beach at a table until her feelings calmed down.

"Tomorrow was week four."

She hoped her life would be better. Briefly, she wondered what Greece looked like. She only saw pictures on the internet. Penelope knew Greece was about a third the size of Montana.

Setting her alarm, she allowed herself time to jog a little before going to work. She looked at the large glass bowl she bought in New York.

"We need to start filling the bowl with shells. A shell for every week that my life gets better. I promised my therapist."

GRAY AREA FOR A WOMAN

Her eyes filled with tears. Her past sometimes hit her when she least expected it. She stopped the wave of emotion. Penelope couldn't go down this road again. She knew her parent's packages were meant to cheer her up.

"The packages did help distract me. The bowl from New York was what set me off. Allan was with me when I purchased the bowl."

16 Corinth, Greece

Thursday Hugh waited for Penelope to finish her restroom break. A call came over his phone.

"Liam, why are you calling me? Is the beach too hot in Corinth? I thought maybe an ancient column fell on you. There's always the canal water. If you drink some, I hear you might have found the fountain of youth.

"Very funny. Seawater isn't good for you. I heard from Carter that there was a fire on Mason Jarett's boat, and it sank in the harbor."

Hugh shook his head.

"We saw the boat last week. The boat was fine."

Liam talked to someone in the room.

"Per Carter, the boat burned last night around midnight. The divers are there this morning getting ready to get in the water."

"I'll talk with Carter," said Hugh.

"What about finding Syd Coogan or Connie Moore? The police should have checked their apartment by now. No one is giving me any information."

"Liam, I've been busy doing my job and your job. The police went to their apartment, and nobody was home. There were food and drinks in the place. They think the couple will return. Some cops are posted and will watch the apartment. There's nothing on the other two women, Beth and Deann."

Liam was frustrated.

"How's Penelope been?"

"She's been busy. We had a nice dinner this past week, and she went to Malibu on Saturday."

"Penelope went to Malibu. Why would she go there? She threw the guy's flowers away."

"Look, pal, she has a life. You have a life."

"Hugh, just get down to Ventura and talk to the divers."

Liam paced back and forth on the cement balcony. His girlfriend joined him. She saw the phone in his hand.

"You called the office!"

"There's been a fire in Ventura. The sailboat next to Duane Hicks's boat caught fire and sunk in the harbor."

"How does the other sailboat affect your case?"

Liam looked at the blue sky.

"Why don't you and your parents eat dinner without me? I think I need to find out more regarding the burned boat."

"All right."

Becka gave him a quick kiss and left. He called Hugh back after two hours. The call went to voicemail. He called Penelope's phone. She answered.

"Hi, Liam, how's Greece?"

"Sunny. Did the divers find anything?"

Penelope bit her lip. Hugh was talking with the divers and the police.

"Yes, they found something unusual."

"A dead body?"

Penelope looked at Hugh who held up two fingers.

She turned away from the scene.

"There are two dead bodies inside the burned boat. I called Mason, and he is fine. He was at home when the fire broke out, or that is what he told the police early this morning. He has no idea who trespassed on his boat and probably caused the fire. When we were here last, the boat windows were closed. I checked. One of the windows shows open."

Hugh approached her. She handed over her phone, so the two men could talk.

"The two bodies are a man and a woman. They might be able to identify them, but it might take a few days. No one saw anybody. One of the other boaters called in the fire. The place is a mess with the gawkers. The boaters on this dock can't get to their boats and are mad at the officials."

"I can imagine. Put Penelope back on."

Penelope took back her phone.

"Are you settled in your apartment?"

Penelope wondered about the switch in subjects.

"My parents keep sending packages, and my surfboard arrived."

"Did you have a good weekend?"

Penelope hesitated.

"I went swimming, jogging, and shopping. I bought two swimsuits."

Liam sat on the balcony ledge looking at the villa's walls. She wasn't going to talk about Malibu.

"Anything else going on?"

Penelope watched Hugh meet their Captain.

"Colleen Brewster turned eighteen and has been released from the detention facility to her mother."

GRAY AREA FOR A WOMAN

Liam wasn't pleased about Colleen being out.

"Her mother is the one that turned her into the facility. This can't be good for the young woman."

"I know. Colleen is like a loose cannon. She could get in serious trouble and never get out of jail. The Captain is here. I need to get back on the job."

"Wait, do the divers have any idea of their age?"

Penelope watched as Hugh motioned for her to join them.

"Call me this evening and I'll fill you in with any further information."

She hung up the phone on him.

"Darn it."

Liam wished he were there. He could hardly leave his vacation. Becka would be angry.

Penelope forgot Greece was ten hours ahead of California. Liam decided to wait a couple of hours and call his boss, Jonathan.

Liam bought a sausage sandwich from a small shop and waited. Finally, he called his boss.

"Hi, boss, tell me what happened in Ventura?"

"Hold on Liam. I'll pull over."

Liam waited. He heard a muffled noise, and the car engine stop.

"The divers found a bracelet on the woman. There were initials *CM*. The man's back of the head showed a partial tattoo. You will never guess who the dead man might be?"

Liam rubbed his face.

"The tattoo was a cougar head."

There was a heavy sigh on the other end.

"Cougar and Connie were on Mason's boat doing what exactly?" asked Liam.

"Good question. You're the investigator on the case. I'll let you figure this one when you return. We have dead fish in a swamp. Of course, we will have to await the official cause of death and identification, but we're confident that gas was somehow used to knock them out, and then the person waited. The killer left a window open to air the boat. Probably an hour later the fire started."

"The killer is sophisticated or very knowledgeable."

The Captain told Liam something else disturbing, but he knew it was a possibility.

"Donnie is out of prison. Let's hope he was nowhere near Ventura last night. I've asked his parole officer to find out."

Liam was now angry he went on this vacation.

"He wouldn't dare take a fire job this soon."

Jonathan was with Detective Carter. Liam could hear Carter speaking.

"Only time will tell. Donnie has the skills but not sure he is a murderer. This job might be a combination," said Carter.

"Did you hear Carter?"

Liam did. He wondered why Carter was with their boss. Jonathan spoke.

"We were at the courthouse to meet an attorney when we heard the call. Since we were this close, both of us checked out the scene."

GRAY AREA FOR A WOMAN

Liam talked a little longer and eventually hung up. His mind was racing when Becka and her parents returned.

After Becka's parents went to bed, she approached him.

"I thought you were going to take a much-needed break."

"I did for almost a week," said Liam.

She put her arms around him.

He did the same. His reaction was automatic.

"You are still far away."

Becka went to bed.

17 Donnie

Donnie Corwin watched the news channel. He flipped back and forth. One of the stations was flickering. There was no cable hookup.

"Aw, this stupid reception is not working."

He torched the sailboat, but the person never told him about the bodies inside. His exhilaration over starting the fire diminished. If the police found out, he would go to jail forever.

The prison officials wouldn't put him with the nice prisoners like Mark. He would get put in with the real bad dudes. Killer man with snake tattoos would not be a good jail mate.

"Two people were on the boat. Stupid me for not checking first. What an idiot? This man conned me into doing the job. I should have asked for more money."

In a panic, he stuffed his clothes into a duffel bag. He wondered where he could go. He sat down on the old mattress. He needed an alibi. Donnie knew he could find someone who wasn't too smart to tell the police he was home.

He needed a drugged-out person or a girlfriend. Donnie stuffed his bag in the ceiling vent. He knew there were plenty of those types of people on the streets. He went outside and walked. There were several questionable people. None of them wore clean clothes. He wasn't going to buy anyone new clothes.

Seeing a young girl that he watched for over an hour, Donnie approached and sat on the park bench.

"Your clothes are clean.

The girl looked at him.

"Forget it. I'm having a bad moment. My life has been nothing but bad moments."

He ignored her. She moved closer and handed him a small candy bar.

"Chocolate."

"Thanks. What's your name?"

The young girl didn't talk again. She pointed to a medic bracelet. He read the name.

"Colleen. I'm Donnie. Nice to meet you."

The girl didn't talk.

"You are allergic to bees."

Colleen showed him her pouch with the medicine.

Donnie nodded that he understood.

"Come on, let's get a taco and a free bottle of water. There's a food truck. We need to act like we are poor. Hold out your hand like this. They will give you water."

The girl followed him.

"Where do you live?"

The girl shook her head.

"You don't remember where you live?"

There was no answer.

"You can live with me from now on. I'll take care of you. No funny stuff. I had enough in prison. You ever been locked up?"

The girl smiled and showed him a tube of lipstick. He opened the tube and touched the pink cream to her lips.

"There you go. Now your lips won't get sunburned."

He bought the sandwiches with coins, and the man gave them free water. They sat in the grass and watched the birds. Donnie enjoyed the quiet. She was perfect for his needs.

He threw away their sandwich papers and stood. The young girl stood. Donnie didn't know if he should command her to stay or let her decide.

"I'm going to my place. You can come or stay here. Your choice."

Donnie walked a block and stopped. He looked at the girl. She was standing in the same place. He saw a policeman looking at her suspiciously. He raced back to her.

"Come on. We have to go before the cop decides to check us out."

The young girl glanced at the cop and put her head down. Donnie took her hand and led her away from the area.

When the parole officer came to visit him the next day, he was surprised to see the young woman. The parole officer questioned Colleen, and she never responded other than to Donnie.

"My girlfriend has been with me since I got out of prison."

The parole officer frowned.

"She appears to be young."

Donnie knew Colleen was eighteen. He showed the parole officer her identification card. The officer read the name, her birthdate, and didn't write it down on his report.

GRAY AREA FOR A WOMAN

After the parole officer left, Donnie wasn't sure what he was going to do with Colleen. She served her purpose. She kept the police from arresting him.

He paced and racked his brain. Maybe he was supposed to keep her a while longer. The girl might be useful. Donnie would need to think carefully about how to proceed. He developed a plan.

Every day he left her and began to lengthen the time he was gone. He brought her magazines and makeup to keep her busy. He encouraged her to grow her hair long and to change her clothes and look. After two months, no one would recognize Colleen Brewster.

He found out she could speak a few short sentences. Donnie encouraged her to talk when he was around. He pointed to the police and kept repeating the word, *danger*. She seemed to understand.

One day she caught him tinkering with a device. She told him the device was dangerous.

Donnie figured out Colleen was smarter than he originally thought. She probably knew he used her to lie for him.

He was careful to build his devices away from the apartment and to hide them in the ground or high inside a partially dead tree.

Any future jobs would not include Colleen Brewster.

He sat thinking about the dead bodies on the sailboat. Donnie didn't dare return to ask the man for more money.

"Not yet anyway. I currently have enough."

He knew the person represented massive evil. Donnie watched the news at night on a stolen television set. The dead man and woman had names and lengthy problems with the law.

"The two dead people weren't exactly the cream of society."

Colleen overheard him and looked at the two pictures on the news screen. She wondered why Donnie was so interested in the couple. She gasped when the police showed a shot of the burned sailboat being taken out of the water.

Colleen freaked out. Donnie immediately clicked the television off.

"Hot, fire is hot. Burn."

"Don't worry. Those people didn't burn. Somebody killed them first. Just the boat burned. The television set shows only pictures. The picture can't hurt you."

Colleen settled down and went back into the kitchen. She returned and handed Donnie his bowl of freshly made popcorn.

"You figured out how to use the popper machine. That's great, Colleen."

"Watch you. Butter melts slowly. Don't touch the burner. Hot."

"You watched me and remembered."

Colleen didn't answer. She was quietly picking the buttered kernels out and eating them first.

Donnie set his half-eaten bowl aside and didn't look happy. He wondered what else she remembered. He found a piece of paper and started to draft a note to the killer. He couldn't spell very well.

"Blackmail is one or two words?"

GRAY AREA FOR A WOMAN

He wrote two words. Then he crumpled the letter and threw it in the trash.

The next morning, Colleen took the paper and hid the writing in her backpack. She could read.

18 DA Visit on Friday

Penelope looked up to see Marvin sit down in her extra chair. Before she could speak, Hugh came around the corner.

"Oops, Mr. Edmond, I didn't know you were here for a visit. How nice? Penelope and I can meet later. Take your time."

Hugh turned to see his boss waving him to the office.

"Excuse me."

Hugh closed the door.

"Jonathan, good morning. This week has been brutal."

"Sit down, Hugh. Explain to me why the District Attorney is here. I don't have anything in my email about a meeting this morning with him."

Hugh shifted in his chair. He knew to play dumb.

"I have no idea either."

His boss squinted his eyes.

"Tell me what you know."

The boss crossed his arms over his chest. Hugh whispered.

"I think he likes Penelope."

"You don't say. I have eyes. I saw the flowers, but usually, he sends me a note. What gives?"

"No clue about who Penelope dates or not. She's an adult. Maybe the swim date didn't go too well."

The Captain frowned. He undid his arms.

"Any news from the lab?"

"Nothing. It's too early. I can call again or drive over there," said Hugh.

"Wait until they are done before you head out."

Hugh nodded with relief.

"You took the words right out of my mouth."

Hugh went to his desk and played with his squeeze ball. An hour later, Penelope appeared.

"Ready?"

"Yes, ma'am."

Hugh grabbed his jacket, and they went to the garage to get their vehicle.

"I'd like to check on Colleen at her mother's place. I looked up the address. Since we are off the schedule, we might as well stop."

"Okay. I'd like to see her again."

They stopped and talked with Colleen's mother and left.

"We'll try the park where her mom dropped her off," mentioned Hugh as he turned the car left at the next corner.

"Can you believe the woman? She left her in the park."

Hugh parallel-parked the car.

"I can believe she dumped her in the hopes her daughter would latch onto someone else. The job they put Colleen in didn't work out. The manager didn't like the lack of her memory. She forgot the correct way to bag groceries. Customers complained when she put the bread on the bottom and the cans on top."

They walked the park grounds.

"I don't see her anywhere. We need to get back to work."

Hugh went to the vehicle.

"There's a sandwich shop close. Let's try there."

Hugh showed the man Colleen's picture.

"Man, we see lots of people. She does look familiar only she was with a guy."

"Can you describe him?"

"Normal height, weight, age early thirties, and he was growing a beard. One spot wasn't working."

The two detectives walked away.

"At least we know Colleen is not alone."

Penelope still looked worried. Hugh tried logic.

"Her mom said she knows how to find her way home. If the guy doesn't work out, she'll be back with her mom. Colleen is eighteen and with her medicine, she should be all right."

"I worry," said Penelope.

Hugh handed her the egg salad sandwich, and he took his roast beef out. They ate in silence. Hugh put his empty wrapper in the bag.

"How did your morning go with the DA?"

Penelope groaned.

Hugh remembered when he dated his wife.

"I get your reaction. Dating is like wandering in the desert. There's a lot of deep sand and prickly stuff."

She smiled.

"Prickly stuff is funny. He wanted to apologize in person."

"Of course, you knew he would."

"I hoped he wouldn't."

GRAY AREA FOR A WOMAN

Hugh watched the ducks walk in the park.

"Will we see flowers on your desk Monday?"

Penelope giggled.

"I suppose. Too bad I gave the fancy crystal vase to Kamilla. I'm now one of her favorite people. I get a cake for my birthday."

Hugh walked to their vehicle. Penelope did the same.

"We have a small bank that wants us to visit them. There's been a strange man coming inside the bank for the last three days. He pretends to fill out a deposit slip and then leaves."

Penelope knew the man was casing the bank.

"Anyone else with the man?"

"They didn't see anyone else. He's probably a loaner. They usually carry guns."

Hugh parked. They were walking toward the bank's lobby when a man with a mask came running out with a bag in his hand.

"What an idiot? He should have taken off the mask. You get the car. I'll chase the lone ranger."

Penelope caught the car keys and unbuckled her gun in one swift motion. Hugh undid his gun while running. She saw the man turn down an alleyway. Penelope started the car and drove over the sidewalks to cut the man off at the other end.

Bringing the car to a screeching halt, she stepped out and held her gun pointed at the man heading toward her. She shouted, "Police, put the gun down now!"

She almost called him a lone ranger. Penelope saw Hugh enter the alley. The man turned and saw he was trapped. He jumped onto a dumpster top and grabbed the fire escape ladder. Climbing to the roof, Hugh watched the man. He ran to the other side of the building.

Penelope made the call to the cops that the bank robber was on the roof. Police cars surrounded the building. Hugh joined her.

"Are we glad there were cars in the neighborhood?"

He was breathing heavily.

"You need to start jogging at night."

They heard gunshots, and the robber shouted that he was giving up. The two detectives waited until the police put the man inside the cage in the back of the police vehicle.

"We can leave. I told you he was a loner."

He waved to the police car.

"I'll turn in the report. Then we can go home."

Penelope drove back to headquarters. She turned the keys over to the attendant.

"I've got to talk to our boss. He sent me a text."

Hugh wasn't sure why the boss wanted to talk to Penelope. He hoped the boss didn't ask her about the pool date. No one at the office was supposed to know. Yet, Hugh told Liam and the boss.

"The review, of course."

He looked at his calendar. She wasn't scheduled for her review for another two weeks.

"Be careful."

Penelope squeezed Hugh's arm.

"I'm always careful."

She went into the boss's office.

"I hear you and Hugh stopped a bank robber today. I wanted to say congratulations."

"Thank you, sir. We seemed to be in the exact spot as the robber. The blues were nearby. Hugh and I couldn't have planned things better."

The Captain was pleased.

"How are you getting along with your team? Any problems or complaints?"

"None, sir."

He looked at her.

"Good. Marvin Edmond told me you were a fine detective. He did stop me in the break room today. Kamilla made a cake. We like her cakes. She does the homemade batter and real frosting. Today was German chocolate with butter pecan frosting. She doesn't put the coconut in. I thought I should let you know about the DA's comment. That's all, detective. Have a nice weekend because Monday, Liam will be back."

"Yes. I'll be ready, sir."

Penelope went to her desk and sunk in her chair.

"Things could get complicated."

There was a piece of cake wrapped in clear plastic on her desk and a note from Kamilla.

"Thank you for the vase."

Penelope undid the wrapping and found the plastic fork. She took a bite. "This cake is the best."

She worried about what was going to be on her desk Monday morning. Marvin asked her if she liked plain milk chocolate.

"I should bring a hammer and a large plastic bowl for all the pieces."

19 Liam's Return from Greece

Liam entered headquarters fifteen minutes early due to hardly any traffic. He was pleased he beat the other detectives for once. He glanced toward Penelope's desk. He didn't see any flowers and was relieved. He noticed something brown and lights twinkling between her large green plant leaves.

"I'm not going to look."

After five minutes, he couldn't stand not knowing. He peeked around the green plant.

"Oh, Geesh."

Liam went back to his desk and chewed on his ballpoint pen. He looked at the pen and threw it in the garbage. He went to Kamilla's desk.

"Hi, Kamilla, I'm back. Do we have anything from the lab?"

"Welcome back, Liam. Why do things happen whenever you leave?"

"I don't know. Lucky, I guess. Nice vase. I hear I missed your cake. You do have my birthday on your calendar."

Kamilla smiled at him sweetly.

"Yellowcake with vanilla pastry on the inside. Powdered sugar sprinkled on the top."

"Correct. Good memory. By any chance, would you know who delivered the chocolate palm tree with the battery mini-lights?"

She brightened.

"Still a sweet talker. You do know deliveries to the detective's desks are private? Detective King is on the force."

"I do. However, you might get poppies today. I hear the florist's shops have them in stock."

"The District Attorney was here unannounced last Friday. Maybe you can figure out the other thing."

Liam's eyes blinked. He recovered quickly.

"Poppies are in order."

Liam went to his desk and made the call to the florist. He ordered two bouquets. Liam walked to the local coffee shop and ordered a salami sandwich. He ate and returned to the bustling office.

On Carter's desk was a huge plastic bowl filled with chocolate pieces. He sauntered over to Penelope's desk. All trace of the palm tree was gone.

"Hello, stranger."

Penelope stood and gave him a quick hug.

"How did you know I like poppies?"

He blushed.

"I got you and Kamilla the same bouquet because you both work hard for me. The flowers are my way of saying thank you."

"I appreciate them. I'm ready."

"Let me get my stuff. Meet you in the garage."

Hugh walked by, stopped, and came back.

"I just realized there was an actual person at your desk. Nice tan, Liam."

Hugh grabbed two large pieces of chocolate.

"You missed this huge palm tree. Chocolate to die for. The twinkle lights were killer magic."

"I like the real palm trees outside better. They sway in the breeze and thrive all on their own."

"No, they don't. The gardening people hired by the city do the watering, and they give them fertilizer twice a month."

Liam was glad to be back. Things didn't change in the office.

"Did you see I bought flowers for my two girls?"

Hugh choked on the piece of chocolate.

"You are the poppy guy? Kamilla and Penelope are your girls. No way."

"I checked. Kamilla has my birthday circled on her calendar. I'm fond of wild poppies."

Hugh wasn't sure Kamilla knew his birth date.

"Dream on. She isn't going to make you a cake."

Liam grabbed a piece of chocolate, made a face, and threw the piece in the garbage. Hugh watched him in disgust.

"The chocolate isn't that bad. It tastes like bunny rabbit chocolate. My kids eat the stuff, and they are alive."

Liam smiled wickedly, "Barely."

Carter came into the office and looked at the two belligerent men.

"I'm allergic to chocolate."

Hugh smiled and moved the chocolate bowl closer to his desk. The twinkle lights were lovingly arranged on the outside of the bowl."

"They look like Christmas."

Hugh went downstairs to visit with Kamilla.

"Any lab results?"

"I'll let you know the half-second they arrive."

He stared at her.

"I have your birthday on my calendar. Your wife said angel food with strawberries."

"I'll bring the whipped cream."

Hugh quickly moved away. The women in the office were touchy and forgetful this morning. First, Penelope whacking the chocolate tree and now Kamilla forgetting the whipped cream. He was safer at home.

Hugh went to the coffee shop and bought a banana muffin for Kamilla. He handed her the bag. She looked inside.

"Thank you, Hugh. I'll make the whipped cream."

"You are welcome, and your whipped cream is better than the canned any day."

Hugh went back to his desk satisfied.

He received a call from Colleen's mom. Colleen evidently came home and took some of her clothes and disappeared again. The mother didn't see her daughter enter or exit the house.

20 Monday Investigation

Liam drove toward Ventura. Penelope knew he wanted to inspect the burned sailboat and talk with the boater who called in the fire.

He looked at Penelope. She looked good. Her skin was getting tan. He realized he missed being around his partner while he was gone.

"What happened to the palm tree from Marvin?"

Penelope looked guilty.

"You saw the tree?"

"I came in early."

She had hoped he wouldn't see the odd delicacy.

"I didn't know bakeries made such a thing."

"This is California. Look around and tell me what you see. I can see clearly."

Penelope looked at the tall buildings and plants.

"Cement."

Liam chuckled.

"Come on!"

Penelope wanted to avoid talking about Malibu with Liam especially while he was driving. She tried explaining.

"He wants to be friends, go to dinner, and be normal. The palm tree was like a joke thing. You couldn't eat the chocolate the way it was."

Liam looked at a bright red fuchsia plant as they drove by.

"Hugh said you have a hammer at your desk."

"Doesn't everyone in the office own one?"

"No, I have a battery-powered screwdriver in my side drawer. Things loosen in the office. I could check your desk for you."

Penelope looked at Liam.

"I missed our little chats. My desk doesn't need tightening. Did you have fun in Greece?"

"Is that why you went out with the DA?"

"No, I only asked about Greece because you hinted about Malibu."

Liam cautioned himself to settle down.

"Yes, for a little while. Greece is beautiful if you are on a honeymoon. I wasn't. Then I worried that you and Hugh were getting all the credit. Nice catch on the bank robber."

They parked and went to the burned boat that was on wooden stilts. A maintenance person brought a ladder. Liam climbed the ladder and took pictures. He moved the ladder several times and took more pictures of the doorway, lock, and open window. When he was done, he thanked the maintenance man.

They walked to the dock, and he took pictures of the scorch marks. There were some cinders on Duane's boat, but nothing that a good wash and a polish job couldn't take care of.

She went with him to talk to the boat owner that called in the fire.

"I was sleeping on my boat. My wife was going to come down in the morning with my daughters. I heard someone shout the word *fire*."

Penelope and Liam knew the last sentence wasn't in the original report.

"Was the voice you heard a man or a woman?"

The man said, "The voice was strange like it was coming from the water. It was a man's voice. I looked in the water and didn't see anything. I looked over the harbor and saw the flames inside the sailboat. I called the fire department immediately."

Liam thanked the man for his time.

"Well, we know this was a murder. I don't need lab results to figure out this scene. The question is why murder these two people? They knew or saw something. Per Connie's friends, the woman only moved when money was involved. Cougar was her pet cat."

Penelope asked Liam, "Did you want to go to the morgue? The autopsy is done. No one has claimed the bodies."

"We'll go. You stay in the car. No need for you to see the bodies twice."

Penelope was glad. She didn't like morgues too much. She stared at the trees. There were lots of palm trees. The bougainvillea's added a splash of color near the small park. The scene was peaceful.

Liam went inside and was gone for twenty minutes.

"Let's do lunch at the soup and salad place."

She thought he would talk about the case. Instead, he wanted to know if he could see her surfboard someday in the future.

"Any time works."

"How about this Sunday? I can come over around ten."

GRAY AREA FOR A WOMAN

"Sunday is good. The rest of my furniture comes Saturday."

They drove to the lab. Liam met with the director. Penelope let him handle the lab people. She stood looking outside as the people walked past. Her phone buzzed.

Hugh gave her an update on Colleen.

"Thanks, Hugh, We're at the lab. Liam's talking with the director. Okay, I'll let you know if he's successful."

Liam came through the door and walked past her. He waited by their car door.

"There were the same wood splinters in their hair. The killer hit them with a board to knock them out, and then took the time to arrange the gas. The fire was started later. There was no reason for the fire. The two dead people were confirmed as Connie and Cougar."

Penelope considered his short sentences.

"If there was no logical reason for the fire, we might have a bigger problem. The fire was for a different purpose. What purpose?"

Liam kicked a rock.

"This was control or spontaneous revenge."

"That's all we need. We have either a confident or an impulsive freak on the loose along with the fire person. How does this fit with Connie's murder?"

"I'll bet I know the name of the fire person."

"Donnie."

"Connie's murder bugs both of us."

Penelope nodded.

"I'm betting revenge on the two bodies."

Liam opened his car door. Penelope sat inside, and they buckled their seatbelts.

"He'll lay low and act like he wasn't part of this fire. Donnie will have an alibi."

"We're going to have to find him," said Liam.

"I don't know if your snitches can."

Liam needed to talk with Hugh.

"There might be someone. He used to work on the force. Hugh might know what happened to Dodge Riskin."

Penelope filed the man's name away in her mind. Dodge was the detective when Donnie was caught and put in prison. They pulled into the headquarters lot. Liam wished he hadn't mentioned Dodge.

"My poppies need to go with me."

Liam went inside. After Penelope left, he stopped by Hugh's desk and waited for him. Hugh dropped his briefcase on his desk.

"Whew. Not much news that we didn't already know."

Hugh sat in his chair with the new pillow form.

"Bad back since the bank robbery. The pillow helps."

He chewed his fingernail. Liam handed him a small nail clipper from his pocket.

"We need to find Dodge."

Hugh handed back the clipper.

"Dodge and I haven't talked in three years."

"I know."

"Our boss won't pay him," said Hugh.

"I'll pay for him. There's one more thing. I'm taking surfing lessons Sunday from Penelope."

Hugh didn't react.

"See you tomorrow."

Hugh looked over where the chocolate bowl stood. The bowl was empty. He placed the empty bowl on Penelope's desk with a smiley thank you note. The twinkle lights he put in a small pile. The battery was worn out.

"I could fix the battery."

Hugh texted Dodge while he put the lights in a plastic baggie.

Dodge called him within minutes.

"Dodge, you kept your old phone number. We haven't talked in ages. How's retirement?"

21 Meeting with Dodge

On Tuesday Penelope waited in the coffee shop with Hugh. They were to meet with Dodge Riskin. A gray-haired man sat down at their table. Hugh introduced Penelope and told him she worked in New York City before Los Angeles.

Dodge listened to Hugh explain the reason they required his help in locating Donnie. The terms of payment were agreed upon. Hugh excused himself leaving Dodge alone with Penelope.

"New York City had a case where a young detective was involved. I have lots of friends in New York, and they told me what happened."

Penelope said, "New York City is a pretty large place."

He nodded.

"I take it no one here knows?"

"The Captain was informed. That is all. I would prefer that you not mention the story. Sometimes things need to remain in the past."

Dodge looked out the window.

"Don't I wish things could remain in the past? Unfortunately, people aren't very forgiving."

Penelope's eyes misted over.

"Excuse me."

He watched her go outside. He tapped his fingers on the table. Penelope was about the same age as his daughter.

Hugh returned.

"Where's Penelope?"

GRAY AREA FOR A WOMAN

"I think she needed some air."

"Yeah, Liam and I have been putting her through pretty fast paces. She's been super and hangs in there. She's tougher than the last two women. Liam is trying this time. I think he's been warned."

Dodge felt for his gun. He was still packing.

"I can imagine that she is super. Women sometimes are a lot stronger. Keep her safe. I believe Liam knows how to handle women."

Hugh watched as Dodge disappeared out the back. He wondered what transpired to make Penelope step outside. He saw her head. Grabbing her coffee, he went to join her.

"You forgot your coffee."

"Oh, thanks. Where do we go now?"

Hugh let the moment go. He almost asked her if she knew Dodge and thought better of it.

"There is a dog we are going to pick up. Dodge requested the dog and will take care of him until we find Donnie. We are to drop the dog at Liam's house. Dodge will get him there."

"A dog for tracking?"

"I think the dog is for catching. A gun isn't effective when lots of people are around."

They received the German Shepherd and drove to Liam's house. The dog sat in the front seat like a human. The dog refused to sit in the back. The rawhide dog bone didn't work. Liam was waiting for them. The dog saw Liam, picked up the dog bone, and came charging out of the car.

"Put the bone down on the step. Good dog."

The dog obeyed.

"I'll walk with him to the beach and back to calm him down."

"Why don't I go with you?" said Hugh.

"The house is open Penelope."

The two men walked the dog on the leash.

"What happened?"

Hugh shook his head.

"I don't know. I left Dodge and Penelope alone. When I came back, she was outside and forgot about her coffee. Dodge said something odd."

"Can you remember?"

"He imagined Penelope was super and women were stronger. He said you knew how to handle women. Dodge doesn't talk that way ever."

Liam knew Dodge.

"Maybe Penelope reminded him of someone."

Hugh almost tripped over the dog's leash.

"I felt somehow Dodge knew who Penelope was. I mentioned New York City."

Liam remembered what the Captain said about Penelope. He was to treat her nicely.

"I'll see if Dodge talks about New York City tonight. I do know some of his friends. Do you think Penelope is hiding something?"

They turned and walked back.

"No. Yes, maybe?"

"She was at your house. Did she talk to your wife?"

"Normal women stuff. We didn't have much time."

Liam wondered.

"Hugh, there is nothing normal about Penelope other than her legs and backside look great in shorts."

Liam started jogging with the dog. Hugh caught up.

"Since when did you see her legs and backside?"

Liam relished the picture in his mind.

"She was ready to go to bed at my place. We talked for about a minute. That one minute was worth the conversation. Soft and nice buns."

Penelope was waiting for them. Hugh took the ice-cold bottle of cola from her.

"Thanks for bringing the dog."

Liam went inside.

"We get to leave."

Penelope tucked her legs in the car.

"The dog looks intelligent."

22 Dog Pick Up

Dodge's old truck barely fit in Liam's small parking space. The backend hung over the sidewalk. Dodge saw Liam waiting in the laundry room doorway.

"I have some burgers ready if you can make the time. The dog probably won't let you leave until you eat. His nose has been twitching since I unwrapped the hamburger."

The dog appeared and dropped his bone in front of the visitor. Dodge threw the bone inside. The dog disappeared.

"Hello, Liam, you look fit. I'll eat burgers. It will be like old times. The house looks impeccably designed. The corner boards all fit."

They sat on the patio off the kitchen cooking while bottled beer was passed around.

"You know Penelope?"

Dodge took a sip of his beer and gave the dog a piece of his hamburger. The question was expected but not quite so soon.

"You never were one to beat around the bush."

Liam turned the burners off and put the plate of hamburgers on the tall bar table out of the dog's reach. Dodge took a burger that was taken off earlier. He threw the burger in the air and watched as the dog caught it.

"Good dog."

Liam waited. There was no pushing for Dodge to respond. The man did things his way always.

"I met Penelope today. She's pretty, young, and nice."

"She came from New York City, and you know lots of people in the law field."

He took a bun and threw it in the air. The dog caught the bun.

"Good dog."

Liam finished his burger.

"I do know lots of people. Some of them are gone. Gone one way or the other."

"What do you know about Penelope?" asked Liam.

"Why do you care? Aren't you dating Becka?"

"Darn it, Dodge, we care. We work with her as partners. Yes, I'm with Becka."

Dodge petted the dog.

"Her daddy knows a lot of people in high places. The file has been closed."

Liam crunched on a pickle and handed the bowl to Dodge. He ate two pickles.

"You need another beer?"

Dodge thought about it.

"Water would be nice."

Dodge broke a hamburger in half and threw the meat in the air.

"Good dog. Last one. Sit."

The dog sat. Liam handed Dodge the water.

Liam had enough time to think in the kitchen.

"People talk. You must have heard something."

Dodge looked at his watch. He should be leaving.

"I heard things. Sometimes you don't know what is real and what isn't. You know how the work world revolves. The world spins. People get caught. Then you look around and figure out who is missing."

Liam looked at Dodge in the dark. Dodge shook his head. Liam knew what he meant.

"She lost someone, and there was more between them," said Liam.

Dodge rose as did the dog.

"I was never here other than to get the dog. I'll let myself out."

Liam took the hamburgers inside along with the empty bottles. He wrapped the burgers in foil and put them in the freezer. The bottles went in the trash.

He ignored the phone call from Hugh.

Liam went to his computer and started looking for newspaper articles. He ran across a few possibilities. Liam shut his computer. There was a detective's name that resonated in his brain.

He called his boss.

"Hi, Liam, why the late call?"

"I need to let you know Hugh and I hired Dodge, and we picked up a dog."

Jonathan hadn't authorized the extra personnel.

"I'll cover Dodge and the dog."

Liam needed to know.

"Dodge has friends in New York City."

Liam mentioned a male detective's name.

There was a noticeable pause.

"Don't interfere, Liam. She was involved with the detective, but she's earned the right to move along."

His boss hung up.

GRAY AREA FOR A WOMAN

Liam knew Penelope earned his respect from the first week.

He answered Hugh's call.

"Well?"

Liam couldn't tell Hugh.

"Dodge was missing his daughter. Penelope reminded him of being young."

"Okay. We wait until Dodge calls us regarding Corwin. I hope he finds the fire creep soon," said Hugh.

Liam put his cell phone down and loaded the dishwasher.

A call came from Becka wanting to know if they were having dinner together Friday night.

"Friday night works. Becka, I'm sorry about being a little off in Greece. The job does take over. Dodge was here. We need his help on a case."

They talked about Dodge for a little bit.

"The man hasn't changed any."

Becka remembered.

"Dodge is deep and tough. He's like you. Easy to love and hard to be around."

Liam input the date on his calendar. He didn't comment.

23 Accidents on the Road

Penelope offered to drive to headquarters. Hugh tossed her the car keys. Their day was over for Thursday. The pavement was hot, and the tires squealed around the corner. Hugh was perspiring while he played with the fan button.

"I told them last week the air conditioner in this car wasn't working correctly. I can tell we have the same vehicle by the missing lighter."

Penelope looked in the glove compartment earlier. The lighter was missing.

"There's a diner five miles ahead. I can stop and get us some sodas with ice. The ice should cool the body."

"Ice is important like air conditioning. We should buy a cooler full."

There was a large green semi-truck in front of her. She looked in her rearview mirror, and traffic was heavy.

"I would try to get around this truck if you can," mentioned Hugh.

There was a pickup next to her boxing her in. His right front fender contained a huge dent. She relaxed her hands and feet.

"I think we are stuck for a little bit."

Suddenly, the pickup truck seemed to stall, and the spot next to her opened. Penelope made her move to pass.

"Lookout, the semi is coming over! Oh, oh, he's swaying. Swaying is bad."

GRAY AREA FOR A WOMAN

Penelope looked at the median and made her decision. She yanked the wheel left and barely missed the back of the swinging green truck. She drove down the center median and saw the highway's only turnaround ahead.

"We'll take the bump and stop in the center of the turnaround road."

Hugh braced himself.

She handled the car like a race car driver and came to a fast stop.

"We should check the car for nicks."

They stepped out, heard tires, horns, and the crunch of metal. They looked at the carnage behind them. The green semi was off to the right bent at an angle, and cars were sprawled all over the road. Hugh looked at their fender.

"Our car is good. We escaped."

They watched as a highway patrol drove toward them in the median. He did the same maneuver as Penelope.

The trouper radioed others. Within minutes two other patrol cars were parked on the turnaround.

"Nice driving. I saw what happened. Unfortunately, other people weren't so lucky or skilled."

"How come we have so many patrol cars in one spot. I thought you guys fanned out." Hugh watched the patrolman.

"We came from a meeting. There are more cars on the way."

They waited for the rest of the patrol cars to arrive, discussed the situation, and watched a few ambulances take an elderly couple to the hospital with breathing difficulty. Other than damages, there was truly little injured at the scene.

The first trooper came over.

"You can leave. We'll take things over from here."

Penelope drove to headquarters. Hugh took his cup of cola and was glad she stopped at the diner. Liam was waiting for them. When she stepped out of the car, he held out his arms. Penelope let him hold her a minute. The accident shook her.

"Where's my hug?" asked Hugh.

The two detectives parted, and Liam gave him a hug and handshake.

"I wouldn't let Penelope drive tomorrow."

She protested.

"I'm glad you both are not hurt. When the trooper said your names over his radio, I became extremely agitated that you might be hurt."

"I need to use the facility."

"Me, too," said Hugh.

Liam watched the two detectives enter the building. He walked around their car. The attendant came to take the car away.

"You might want to check the alignment," said Liam.

The attendant saw the grass on the bumpers.

"I've tried to get them to buy the higher vehicles. They won't change them out unless we wreck them. The air conditioner blinks on and off on this car. We think there's a short somewhere. Our best mechanic can't figure out the car. I'm thinking she's a lemon. No lighter either is a bad sign."

Liam wondered at the logic of their current maintenance plan. He remembered the license plate number. He didn't want to drive the car in the future.

24 Captain Meeting

Penelope saw the note on her desk Friday morning. Hugh and Liam were in the boss's office. She hurried into the room.

Jonathan looked at his three detectives.

"A pickup driver said our car bumped his vehicle on the highway yesterday."

Penelope raised her hand.

"Not to worry, we have a patrolman who saw the whole thing. Penelope didn't change lanes until after the red pickup drove off the road due to a flat tire. The department is glad our two detectives chose the median when the green semi-truck swerved. He swerved to avoid hitting an elderly couple who were driving too slow."

Liam looked at his hands. The accident could have ended badly.

"Liam, where is Dodge in your case."

"Dodge does things his way. He is methodical. As soon as he has any inkling regarding Donnie's whereabouts, he will call."

The Captain looked at Hugh.

"Nothing further on the two victims. There is a week where no one saw them."

Jonathan stood. He looked at his large whiteboard.

"Has anyone contacted Beverly Hicks recently?"

Liam breathed out some air.

"Penelope and I will make a call on Monday."

GRAY AREA FOR A WOMAN

"Why can't you go today? Hugh, I know your kid has a dental appointment."

Liam passed a piece of paper to his boss. He read the contents.

"Pomona has found Beth Sand's whereabouts and is holding her at the jail. Good. Perhaps she can shed some light on the three ladies, and what they were doing with Madeline Foster. She might also know what Cougar and his girlfriend, Connie, were up to. Their deaths created this mess of a case. Hugh and Penelope, you are dismissed."

The detectives left the meeting and huddled around the coffee machine in Penelope's cave.

"Do you feel like we just got excluded from some club? Beth Sand is big news."

Penelope watched Hugh select the coffee grounds.

"Paranoia is never a good sign."

"I'm not paranoid. Is this the coffee we drank yesterday?"

Penelope pointed to the correct bag. Hugh made the coffee and poured them a cup.

Hugh tried to look through her plants.

"What kind of fertilizer are you using? These plants have grown. They are still talking in the boss's office."

Penelope stirred in the dried cream.

In Jonathan's office, the boss looked at Liam.

"Are you cool with working with Penelope, or would you like to be reassigned?"

Liam swallowed.

"I'm fine. I needed to know the scoop on Penelope and did some research. I won't be blindsided if she freezes."

"Hugh?"

"He doesn't know."

Jonathan took his glasses off.

"She won't freeze. On the stakeout, she did her job. The DA doesn't know either, not that it would matter to him."

Liam could smell the fresh coffee.

"Sunday, Penelope is teaching me to surf. I'll probably fall flat on my face."

The Captain was relieved his detectives could relax.

"Keep me updated on Ms. Sand."

Liam went to his desk and downloaded the worksheet for today. Penelope waited for him.

When they arrived at the jail, they talked with Beth Sand. She confessed the four women planned on going on a trip with Duane Hicks on his sailboat to Mexico.

"Deann thought the trip was a vacation. The plan was to steal his sailboat. We didn't."

"Who changed the plan?"

"I thought Madeline did."

Liam watched the woman.

"We talked with Madeline."

Beth shuffled her feet.

"Maybe Connie did."

"You haven't heard about Connie and Cougar?"

The jailed woman frowned. Her fingernails tapped on the table.

"I've been hiding in my mom's basement. Her television is broken. I got scared and told them I was on the forty-five-foot boat. It wasn't my idea. I get sick on boats. I should have stayed home. I would have except Madeline gave me money. She said I owed her, and she would go to the police if I didn't go. She forced me. The police must understand. I'm not the guilty one. She's the person with the big ideas, and she's cruel."

Liam rubbed his right eye. Someone was very cruel.

"They are both dead."

Penelope watched the woman panic.

The woman spread her hands open.

"Who is dead?"

Penelope spoke softly, "Connie and Cougar are dead? They were gassed and later burned."

Liam knew Beth also wasn't informed by the others.

"Mrs. Hicks was in on the stealing of her husband's boat. Connie didn't come right out and say the words. She hinted. I don't know if there was a second plan. There could have been."

Liam shook his head.

"I don't believe you. Mrs. Hicks owned the boat with her husband. There's no reason to steal the sailboat. Duane likes his boat, but he could always buy one bigger."

"Connie told me, I swear, and now she's dead. I didn't do anything but get on a stupid sailboat. I'm never getting on a boat again."

Liam rose.

"I'm going to step out for a few minutes and talk with my partner."

Liam and Penelope stepped out of the room and went outside onto the large cement area.

"Can we just leave and go to the beach?"

Penelope leaned on the metal railing. The day was warm, and the railing was cool to the touch. She looked at the large Sycamore trees.

"We seem to be going in loops."

"Madeline was the leader or was Connie the leader?" asked Liam.

Penelope wondered.

"We now have a finger pointed at Mrs. Hicks. Is the finger-pointing because no one knows who was in control?"

Liam shoved away from the railing.

"We take Beth's statement, and she will be charged with the same crime as Madeline. We know she was involved as an accessory in that theft. Beth admitted as much. She hasn't implicated anyone else. Monday, we visit Mrs. Hicks."

Penelope wondered about something Beth mentioned.

"Madeline uses people. I wonder how many others she has used?"

Liam stared at the Sycamore tree.

"The bark turns a nice pink color after rain. Do you want me to come over Saturday to help with the furniture workers and show them where to put the stuff?"

"Thanks, but no thanks. I've got the furniture covered."

He could hardly wait until Sunday.

"I could come an hour earlier. I bought a rubber suit in case the water was cold."

Penelope needed to feel the ocean water rushing past. There was freedom riding the surfboard.

"Sure. Bring some gooey rolls or filled ones."

"You got it."

They went inside the jail and finished their interview. Penelope went home early, and Liam informed the Captain about the jail interview. Liam found out Donnie missed his second parole check-in. The police rechecked the place he was staying.

Liam and the Captain figured Donnie was running from someone. He hadn't appeared at any of his old haunts. They figured out who Donnie was running with. A metal medic bracelet was found in the bathroom on the tub ledge in an apartment.

Liam let Hugh know the name on the medic bracelet. Hugh checked again with Colleen's mother. She hadn't seen her daughter since she left. Her clothes were the same in the closet. A jar of popcorn and a stick of butter was missing from the house.

Both men decided not to tell Penelope until necessary. Otherwise, she would go looking for Colleen instead of getting her furniture delivered.

Liam wanted to keep the surf date.

25 Surf Lesson

Penelope answered her call from the front desk. The visitor was given clearance to enter the elevator. The security guard let him pass. She met Liam in the hall and helped carry his suit into her apartment.

She took him on a tour of the completely decorated rooms.

"This place has been transformed. Nice job."

They sat down and ate cream cheese filled rolls and juice.

Penelope changed into her suit, and he used the den to change into his suit. They went downstairs and retrieved the surfboard from the locker cage.

Showing Liam some techniques on the sand, they moved into shallow water. After an hour, she thought he was ready for a ride.

"You stay here on the board, and I'll get us ready to catch a wave. Watch when I move."

After a couple of rides together, she told him he was ready. They reversed positions. A wave came in, and they both paddled. Liam stood up and tried to balance and hang onto Penelope. They both fell over.

They tried for another hour, and then she let him handle the board by himself. After three decent tries, he came floating over to her.

"I'm sure beat. Teacher, I need to stop and float like a dead man."

They stuck the board in the sand on the beach. They went back into the water. Liam floated, and she floated next to him. He grabbed her hand, so she didn't float away.

"This is why people like California. Sun, surf, and miles of water. Not to mention palm trees and sexy women in bikinis."

She splashed him.

Liam stood up in the water and came closer to Penelope.

"You look different all wet."

The sun was in her eyes. She didn't see him get close, and he kissed her on the lips. He turned her so she could see him.

"Liam, I don't know what to say. We work together. Kissing in the water is sacred or dangerous."

"I know. We won't be able to see the sharks. Sorry, I got carried away by the moment. Your lips were begging to be kissed. We should get out of these wet swimsuits."

They trudged up the beach with the board and put it back in the locker.

Liam and Penelope changed in the condominium. She wore a soft peach pantsuit. He was in khaki shorts and top.

"Would you like something to drink?"

"Any soda will do."

She brought out two bottles. They sat at her counter and drank the cold liquid.

"I enjoyed the lessons today. I didn't realize how many muscles surfers use. My knees are wobbly. The board must have bumped me a hundred times."

Penelope was thinking about floating in the water.

"Could we do that thing again?"

Liam looked at her.

"Which thing?"

Penelope put her cola on the countertop and slid over. She kissed him on the lips. Liam knew he was in trouble. He willingly kissed her back and was surprised when she moved away.

"I wondered how you kissed. The first time was good, but I wasn't prepared. The second one was passable. Now I know."

Liam wasn't sure where his next move should take him. They were in dangerous territory. He thought his kiss was better than good. Passable meant what exactly.

"Passable like in a P grade. No way. I kiss better than acceptable."

Liam wasn't going to let her get away with the slam. He reached for her. She scrambled out of the stool and ran for the cover of the lounge chair. He tried to move the chair.

"You owe me another try."

She screamed as he grabbed her and gave her a better kiss.

He stopped.

"Well, I do get a better grade. My kiss was exceptional."

She smiled sweetly and touched his collar.

"Three kisses. I bet myself you would play into my hands.

Liam couldn't believe her.

"I fell for the third kiss attempt.

She nodded.

Liam took her in his arms. He kissed her more slowly.

"I bet on four."

She looked startled. She decided on their next move.

"Funs over. I'll help you with your gear."

She walked him to the elevator. Penelope handed him a bag.

"This is a gift to put in your kitchen."

Liam looked in the bag.

"Hugh told me they were the best hot pads. Thanks!"

He smiled at her as she waved. The door closed. Liam sighed. He thought things were going well between them.

"She's shed a whole different light on surfing."

Liam stored his gear in his sports car and drove halfway home. He pulled over and thought about his morning with Penelope. Something was happening between them.

He drove to the office and sat at his desk. Liam doodled on a piece of paper with the names of all the players in the current case. He kept staring at the names and the dates. His head filled with conversations and interviews.

"She's right. We've been going in loops."

He picked up his phone.

She answered right away.

"Hey."

Penelope was glad he called.

"Hey back."

"I'm at the office. You are right. I see the loops."

"Monday should be interesting with Mrs. Hicks."

"Were those real antlers in your parent's room? Even the pillow looks like the buttons were made from horns."

"Yes. Antlers and horns are plentiful in Montana."

"Crazy. Today was fun," said Liam.

Penelope smiled. Surfing and kissing games were fun. She even surprised herself with her rash behavior. Surf, sun, and Liam were a situation requiring more control than she counted on. She questioned why she wore the bikini.

"I enjoyed the day."

Liam rang off and went home. He took a long shower and looked at the bruises on his legs.

"Ouch, I've never seen anything so ugly."

26 Beverly Hicks

Hugh watched Penelope print the day's schedule for Monday. She tossed the schedule into a folder.

"I like to keep the paper version for records."

"Isn't this your sixth week with us?

Penelope checked her calendar.

"The beginning of the sixth."

"What did you do with Liam? He's hobbling around like an old man. I know he's in pain, but he's smiling. Drugs are prohibited in the office unless there's a prescription."

"I haven't seen Liam yet. He's probably getting an egg breakfast at the deli. We spent a good three hours or more surfing. I should have kept the lessons to a limit of two hours. I thought he was tougher. High doses of aspirin are allowed in the office."

"No, he's old like me. The tough part is all show when women are around."

Hugh sucked in his stomach.

"See."

Penelope was tired. The furniture delivery and Liam wore her out.

"I'm a little tired today. No jokes. I could have used another day off."

Hugh looked at her strangely.

"I'm tired from surfing, Hugh. He did like the hot pads."

Liam stood at her desk. He looked at Penelope. She blushed and he blushed. She spoke.

152

"I have to leave. My old and frail partner is here."

Hugh stood.

"Can I see your bruises?"

Liam punched Hugh lightly on the arm.

"Ow. I guess not. Have fun kids. Stay out of the water."

Liam smiled at his female detective for the day.

"I'll show you my bruises."

She punched him as she went past.

Hugh rolled his chair out.

"I heard that comment."

Liam shoved Hugh back into his desk.

The two detectives were outside.

"It's such a glorious day, I'll drive my car. You can look at the trees," said Liam.

Penelope looked at the blue sky.

"What can go wrong?"

They drove to Beverly Hicks's home. The yard looked manicured. They pressed the front door buzzer.

No butler was answering the door. Liam walked around to the side gate and undid the latch. The pool didn't look like it had been cleaned in a while. Liam came around the front.

"The doors are locked, and I didn't see anyone through the patio door. There are cars in the garage. The odd part is the pool. It's loaded with leaves."

"Should we call the police?"

Liam looked around the neighborhood and saw a car across the street.

"Let me ask the neighbor."

GRAY AREA FOR A WOMAN

Penelope watched as Liam talked with the owner. She tried to see inside the foyer. The foyer was empty. There was no mailbox other than the large metal boxes together at the corner. She looked and saw no newspapers or flyers.

Liam returned.

"I've called the police. They have called the security company."

The police opened the front door, and the security company turned off the alarm. Penelope and Liam waited while the police checked the house. A second police car arrived, and the officers went inside.

The first officers appeared.

"We have a dead body on the first floor and a second one on the second floor."

Liam called their boss. He came back into the house and talked to the officer. Penelope waited outside.

When he returned, Liam told her Mrs. Hicks was dead and he thought the man was the pool person."

Penelope asked, "How?"

"Gunshot."

"Suicide?"

Liam rolled his eyes.

"My answer would be negative. There were marks all over the wall safe. The murderers were unsuccessful in getting inside the safe. There might be expensive jewelry missing from an empty dresser drawer."

"We have a messed-up robbery. How long do we have to stay here?"

"We'll wait until the coroner arrives. We can sit in my car."

They sat for ten minutes.

"I hope the bruises aren't too bad."

Liam told her he put some salve on them just to be safe. He wrapped his knees with stretchy bandages for support.

"Is that what I smell?"

"Here's the coroner's vehicle. Let me give him my card. Don't move."

Penelope waited. The coroner and a woman grabbed their bags and talked with Liam. She thought about the bodies in the house. Beverly's elegant home would be sold. The buyers wouldn't know what happened inside unless they talked with the neighbors. She remembered how vibrant Beverly seemed. The deaths seemed senseless. He jumped in and backed out of the driveway.

Liam drove easily on the freeway to headquarters.

They went inside. The Captain was driving to the office to meet them.

Liam received a call from Dodge. He sent him a picture of Donnie and Colleen running on some railroad tracks.

He read the text.

"They disappeared. I think a car picked them up. I stayed back. They didn't see me."

Liam went into Penelope's office space and told her about Colleen Brewster.

"Oh, no. Donnie is not someone she should be around. This is bad. How in the world did he connect with her? The park. Her mother left her at the park."

"We'll try to find them. Dodge is still looking."

Penelope couldn't stop thinking about the timing of their interview.

"I wonder if we should have gone to Mrs. Hicks's home on Friday?"

Liam saw a lot of dead bodies. He knew the two people were dead for some length of time.

"They were already gone."

Penelope thought about insurance money.

"Thirty million."

Liam wondered.

"Hard to collect if you are missing."

Hugh came running toward them.

"You saw them?"

Liam nodded.

Hugh dragged a chair over and sat down. He wanted to be part of the team.

"How dead?"

"Gunshot a while ago. They were in different rooms. She must have screamed for the pool man to come inside the house," said Liam.

"Insurance," mentioned Hugh.

"We're riding the same boat. We need to see the timeline."

Hugh agreed with Liam.

The Captain arrived with boxes of pizza.

"My office. Some corporations paid Madeline Foster's bail a couple of days ago. She has disappeared and so has the shell corporation. We have work to do."

Penelope watched Hugh leave her desk.

"I'll be a few minutes. I must cancel a dinner engagement."

Liam knew her dinner partner, and he left with a strange look on his face. He went into the boss's office.

"Where's Penelope?" asked Jonathan.

"She's canceling her dinner date with Marvin Edmond."

The Captain replied, "Oh. I'm sure they can reschedule. The Chief wants a review tomorrow. Let's eat. The pizza tastes better hot."

Hugh piled several pieces on his paper plate. Jonathan took cold water out of his small refrigerator and passed the bottles around.

In five minutes, Penelope appeared. She took a cheese slice of pizza.

Liam finished his meat slice and stared at his water bottle.

"Let's begin."

When they were done, all the players were on the whiteboard.

"Thoughts?"

Hugh yawned and spoke.

"We need to know when our latest victims died. The chart is important, but these last murders might have changed our first guesses."

The Captain looked at Penelope and Liam. There was no comment from either one. Hugh shrugged his shoulders. One minute the two people were talking, and the next minute they weren't talking.

"We also need to find some missing persons."

GRAY AREA FOR A WOMAN

He drew several empty boxes on the whiteboard.

"Go home everyone and keep thinking. We need answers."

The three detectives left the boss's office.

Penelope went to her sports car. Liam followed her. She stopped.

"I'm sorry. Sometimes I get overly stressed plus my legs hurt."

"Hugh didn't say thirty million dollars. He said insurance."

"I caught the inference."

Penelope watched Liam. She shook her head.

"Madeline started this project, and there's one person we haven't met nor seen."

"Deann. You think they might be the leaders rather than Mason or Duane. We're still looking at Duane. Mason is a longshot. We're not sure how he would gain."

"We have no proof. I think there were a lot of errors made by others. The greed scale seemed to have hit the players in the game like a bad virus. However, if we can't get the two women for the first project, we can keep them in prison for the second stolen boat project. Tomorrow we can talk. I'm tired, and I'm sorry about your legs. I'll be gentler next time."

"There's a next time."

Penelope needed to correct her last statement.

"Surfing."

Liam was also exhausted, and his nerves were frayed. He went to his car.

He waited until she drove away.

"At least she's not mad at me. I wonder why she doesn't want any more kisses."

27 Visit Mrs. Brewster and Dodge

Penelope and Hugh drove to the home of Colleen's mom. The house was small and needed paint. The stucco was faded and looked faintly purple in the morning light. There were no plants on the place, and the driveway was gravel. A lizard ran under a large rock.

The day was Tuesday. The woman had Tuesdays off. She opened the screen door. The house smelled of fried eggs and toast. Dirty dishes were on the kitchen counter.

"I haven't cleaned the place yet."

They talked with her in the sparse living room. Hugh explained her daughter was with a man who more than likely started a fire. The police were looking for him because he skipped out on reporting to his parole officer.

"My daughter wouldn't stay with someone like this man. She is afraid of fire and bees. She panics."

Penelope handed over Colleen's medic bracelet.

"We found her bracelet in an apartment where Donnie Corwin was staying. He's the man in your daughter's life."

The mother appeared upset but put the bracelet on the window ledge over the kitchen sink.

"She needs her bracelet. If she comes back, she will put the bracelet on her arm," said Mrs. Brewster.

They encouraged the mother to contact them if she heard or saw her daughter. Or if the bracelet disappeared, Hugh should be contacted. They left the house.

Penelope was glad to be out in the fresh air. The house was depressing.

"Where are we going? The schedule shows blocked off."

Hugh drove to the Pomona jail.

"We're visiting Dodge. After Liam called me last night and told me about your conversations, we decided Dodge could be more useful in a cell next to Beth. My family has his dog in our fenced backyard. The kids have food, play, and poop detail."

Penelope could imagine the kids taking care of the dog. They entered the jail room, and a handcuffed Dodge was brought inside. The guard undid the cuffs.

"Hello, Penelope and Hugh. I needed a break and a shower, so I checked in for a week. The soap they used three years ago was nicer. I assumed budget cuts. The wrist jewelry that I'm wearing is the same."

"Very funny. Any clue where we might look in Mexico?"

"Beth mentioned how she loved to go to Cancun for vacation. When I asked her if she had friends there, she clammed up."

Hugh looked worried.

"I told her that I used to live there a long time ago which I did. I've talked about my buddies and fishing stories. I put her to sleep. At this point, I'm gaining her confidence."

"Any other cities she mentioned?" asked Penelope.

"She did say she liked to go to San Diego. Her parents owned a house. There was a dirt road, and she was responsible for getting the mail every day. She complained the sand was hot, and she was afraid of the large cats."

Hugh wrote in his notebook.

"We have some information. This should be helpful. Do you want us to spring you out?"

Dodge thought about it.

"No, the food is surprisingly good, and we have a volleyball tournament this Friday. I think Friday after four works for me. If I find out anything more, I'll be in touch."

The two detectives rose to leave.

"Who's Deann?"

Penelope and Hugh sat down. Beth talked about Deann to Dodge.

"She's one bad female along with Madeline. They were going to steal Duane Hicks's boat but chose a different boat. The different boat was a forty-five-footer for the trip on the water to Mexico. Her whole crew was greedy. Some of them are dead and Duane's still missing. We think Deann is with Duane. He might or might not have a clue about the danger he is in. The game is a high stake's life insurance."

Dodge assessed the information Hugh provided.

"Sailboats and bad broads. We also have Donnie in the mix. Fireworks ahead. I'll see what is in Cancun. She mentioned a ski boat and a dive school. I would imagine Duane knows how to dive. I doubt he skis."

The guard put the handcuffs back on and escorted Dodge from the room. The detectives went to their vehicle.

"We should be able to find the San Diego house from the tax records."

Hugh stopped at the traffic light.

"I'll contact the Cancun authorities with the Captain's help. We'll check the ski shops, dive shops, and restaurants close by."

He pulled onto the freeway.

"How did you and Liam put the two women together? I was way off base."

Penelope thought about the interview with Madeline.

"Deann's name was mentioned last, but it was the way she said her name. You or I would say the name fast. She said, Dee Anne. She made a point of correcting Liam when he read her written note of the names for the women."

"Maybe we have the spelling wrong. Her first name might be Dee for Deirdre. I'll ask Carter to run the name through the system differently."

Penelope remembered something.

"There's also the ski place in Squaw Valley to remember. If Duane is alive, he'll want to keep the place or sell the asset."

Penelope answered her phone. Liam talked with her. She turned toward Hugh.

"Beverly and her pool person were killed before the fire on Mason's boat."

Hugh watched the freeway.

GRAY AREA FOR A WOMAN

"One loop closes. Why do they make things complicated? It's obvious Connie and Cougar killed Beverly and the pool guy. Who ordered the hit, or did they make their own decision? Mason now gets insurance money from the burned boat. He probably could have sold the boat and received the same amount. How does Mason fit with Connie and her boyfriend? He can barely walk."

Penelope pondered the questions.

"Did anyone contact Mason's doctor?"

Hugh swerved off a ramp and dialed Liam.

"Check out Mason's doctor. When could he walk?"

Hugh figured out the first loop.

"Duane and Mason talked with Madeline about sailing. There is a connection to Connie. That was a huge mistake. The second mistake was connecting with Beverly. Mason might be the man. He could be the one Duane complained about as a mysterious lover. Beverly and Duane argued a lot. Mason and the affair with Duane's wife make more sense instead of the pool guy."

Penelope looked at the cars on the freeway. A mother was driving her children to a birthday party. She could see the balloons and presents in the back window.

"We three detectives work well together. The fault was the distrust in the marriage. Of course, Madeline targeting Duane's boat was the beginning of bad news."

Hugh drove down the ramp.

"Madeline was the catalyst. We're sure Duane is in Mexico?"

Penelope responded, "Absolutely. Lake Tahoe would have been my second guess. I don't think he went to San Diego. San Diego is too close to LA."

"When I get home, I'm going to tell my wife that I love her immensely."

"And the dog."

"Oh, man. I almost forgot. I've got to stop and get a bag of dog food. He already ate the bag Dodge gave us."

Penelope frowned.

"How could the dog eat so much?"

"We put the food in one of those glass tower things."

Penelope laughed.

"No, wrong idea. You are only supposed to give them the measure cupful of dry food in the morning and the evening."

Hugh looked like he dropped the ball.

"Is that why there was a cup? I threw the darn cup away."

"I'm sure you can get one at the pet store. Why don't we stop? I'll help plus we need a large metal bowl."

"My kids have a bucket of water they fill."

"The bowl is for the dry dog food."

"The plastic ones are cheaper."

He glanced at Penelope who was shaking her head.

"Right. This dog eats plastic. Good thing my fence is wood," chuckled Hugh.

"We should stop and get a few pounds of hamburger," said Penelope.

"I'm not buying a dog pricey hamburger."

"Do you like your fence?"

Hugh looked shocked.

"I have to keep this dog until Friday. I'm going to kill Dodge."

Penelope saw the grocery store next to the pet store. Hugh pointed.

"Look, we can save time. I'll get the pet junk, and you buy the cheap hamburger. Get the 60/40."

"They don't make those percentages."

"The butcher can if you ask."

They both disappeared and came back to the car with their bags.

"You bought hamburger buns?"

Penelope smiled.

"Liam said the dog likes the buns. He behaves well after eating buns."

"That's not the only buns he likes."

Penelope overheard him.

"What?"

"Nothing. I didn't say anything. Soft buns are fine."

They stopped by Hugh's house and dropped off the bags. Penelope visited with Emma while Hugh changed out the containers. He checked his fence before they left and threw the new frisbee for the dog.

On the way to the office, Penelope was quiet. Hugh's family and home were exciting to be around. No wonder Hugh hurried home in the evening. There was joy surrounding his family.

"The store guy told me the frisbee was indestructible."

"He lied," said Penelope. She bit her finger to keep from saying anything further.

"Oh, for crying out loud. There are going to be holes in the frisbee. Well, the spoiled dog won't eat so much hamburger. I saw you bought the 85/15 meat."

"The butcher recommended the package. He gives his Bernard dog the same stuff."

"You mean St. Bernard. I'm never getting a big dog, a medium dog, or a little one."

28 Mirror Glass

Wednesday at three in the afternoon, Hugh was driving through an alley in Los Angeles. She looked at her phone screen to read the call record.

"The woman complained about a bum climbing in her garbage container outside her restaurant."

Hugh looked at the GPS map.

"I thought we would drive through the back and get the lay of the land. There's the dumpster."

Hugh and Penelope stepped out of the car and walked around the large green bin. The bin was dented and rusted. Hugh peeked inside.

"Everything looks familiar to me. There's garbage inside. We'll go around the front of the restaurant. We can receive the complaint from the owner, check off the call record, and be finished. Easy."

They knocked on the restaurant door. There were four tables with chairs outside in a wooden gated area.

"Outside dining."

Hugh knocked again. No one answered, and the place was dark inside. He tried the lock, and the lock held. Hugh called Kamilla to confirm they had the correct address.

Hugh looked at the number above the restaurant and the street sign.

"We are in the right place. Can you try calling the owner? Don't call the number that came in. We'll wait."

After five minutes, Kamilla called Hugh.

"The owner said she never submitted the complaint. The restaurant hired a guard for when they are open. They haven't had any problems. I'll put the call down as bogus."

"Thanks, Kamilla."

Hugh looked around the outside of the restaurant and down the street. People were coming and going. Nothing seemed unusual or out of place.

"We get weird calls, but this one seems particularly odd."

They walked back to the car and climbed inside. Penelope was putting on her seatbelt. Halfway down the alley, a shotgun was fired and broke their back windshield. The glass shattered loudly. Penelope felt a slight prick.

"Creep, he knows a pistol wouldn't break the glass as easily."

Hugh backed up the car until he saw a man with a shotgun in his hand running down the street. Hugh jumped out and ran after the man. Penelope got out and was going to turn the car around. She noticed the mirror inside was broken.

She slid into the driver's seat. Racing down the alley in the car, she saw Hugh. There was a man on the ground with handcuffs on. The shotgun was nowhere around.

"He threw the shotgun in the bushes. I bet he only was given one bullet."

Penelope wondered at the comment.

A police car pulled in behind her, and they took the man away. The shotgun was retrieved for evidence along with the empty shell casing. Penelope let Hugh drive back to headquarters.

Hugh got out of the car. Penelope didn't move in the passenger seat.

"Hugh, take me to the emergency room, I'm bleeding."

"Where? Oh, god."

He saw the red blood on her blouse. Hugh scrambled into the car and drove her to the emergency room. The nurses disappeared with her on a cart.

"What is happening? Where are you taking my partner?"

"She has mirror glass in her neck. She needs x-rays and possibly surgery," hurriedly said the nurse.

Hugh knew mirror glass was the worst. He leaned down and whispered to Penelope.

"Don't die on me or I'll get in deep trouble with Emma."

Penelope squeezed his hand. Hugh was more afraid of his wife's reaction than their Captain.

After he was notified that they were taking her into surgery to remove the silvered glass, he called his boss. Then he called his wife.

Hugh went to the hospital gift shop and selected a stuffed monkey.

After three hours, she was released, and Hugh drove her home. They stopped and received her medicine from the pharmacy. Hugh found the wheelchair, and they rode the elevator to her floor.

"Nice condominium. I'll have Liam drive your car over tomorrow. You rest. Oh, here's a gift for your office."

Hugh left. Penelope took her pills with water and found some soup to eat for dinner. The microwave heated the soup. She ate half the noodles and dumped the rest. She stumbled down the hall and crawled onto her bed.

In the morning, she was hot and achy. Penelope grabbed an orange juice, found some crackers, and took her pills.

She sat in the lounger in the living room. Her phone rang. The call was from Liam.

"I'll be there in ten minutes. I've got your car. I'll take a taxi to the office. How are you feeling?"

"Like I fell off my surfboard and drowned twice before rolling up on the beach with the dead shark who caused the crash. I can't even take a shower without plastic. Who has plastic that large?"

"Sounds bad. I'll stop and get free shower caps from a hotel chain I use. We can tape them together. Hang tight."

"Shower caps. I might have some in the guest bedroom."

"Don't move until I knock. I'll find the shower caps."

29 Second Emergency - Infection

She let Liam into her condominium.

"Hi, stranger."

Liam gently hugged her. He saw the large gauze bandage on her neck.

"Can I look at your stitches?"

She stood still holding the counter while he pried the tape off her neck. Liam looked at her flushed face. Her eyes were overly bright.

"Where's your thermometer?"

She pointed toward her bedroom.

"Bath cabinet."

He glanced around the master bedroom and saw the door to the bath. He brought back the thermometer and stuck it in her mouth. He pulled the object out and read the digital screen.

"Too high. I'll get a wheelchair from the lobby. You are going to the hospital. The stitches and the surrounding area look blue. They shouldn't be big and puffy."

Liam sat in the emergency room. The doctor came out to talk with him.

"Good thing you brought Ms. King into the ER. We found another sliver of the mirror. The piece has been removed. We're going to keep her overnight and get some fluids inside. I want to make sure the infection recedes. We've drawn lines on her skin. You should be able to take her home Friday morning if the infection is contained."

172

Liam drove back to Penelope's condominium and stayed overnight. He checked the refrigerator to make sure she had food. At ten o'clock in the morning, he drove to the hospital to get her.

Depositing her in the lounge chair, he put the wheelchair outside the door.

"Look, I'm staying overnight to make sure you are all right. I promised the doctor that someone would stay with you. Don't argue. It's settled."

Penelope took the pills and water. She fell asleep. Liam touched her forehead. He called Hugh to let him know her status.

"Are you crazy? You can't stay overnight in her condominium. What about Becka?"

Liam ran his fingers through his hair.

"She'll not know until I tell her. Unless you want to stay overnight with Penelope? I promised the doc."

Hugh watched his wife clear the kitchen table.

"I've got the wife, kids, and a spoiled dog who eats hamburgers with soft buns. You owe me a couple of boards of wood fencing. I can't stay with her. What about her parents?"

"She doesn't want her parents to know she has been injured. I can't blame her. Penelope's dad is very protective. Her mom would rush out and buy her more clothes. Therefore, I'm it for today."

"There's always Marvin."

Liam wasn't going that route.

"No!"

"Okay, just don't do anything," said Hugh.

Liam was exasperated.

"I'm a detective. She's my partner. I'm a nice guy. I respect her."

Hugh knew Liam would take care of Penelope. He also agreed with the man.

"What am I supposed to tell the Captain?"

Penelope opened her eyes.

"Liam?"

"Hugh, I've got to go. She is awake. Don't worry. Things will be fine. I'll get her to contact our boss."

Liam went over and sat in the other lounger. He handed her an apple juice.

"Hugh is worried about you. You should also check in with the boss."

Penelope knew her forehead wasn't so hot anymore. She was going to get well.

"I'm glad you didn't contact my parents. Is there any way we can have Kung Pau Chicken? The oatmeal was paste. I couldn't swallow the stuff. I'm getting hungry."

Liam dialed the restaurant number.

"Twenty minutes. They are doing a special delivery. He mentioned the restaurant's name. They don't usually open until three."

She held out her hand. He gently kissed it.

"I'm glad you are staying. I needed a friend."

Liam was glad she was feeling better.

"I've got to make a call. I'll wait downstairs in the lobby for the takeout."

She watched him leave. Penelope dialed Jonathan to let him know she might take Monday off.

He told her to take all the time she needed. After twenty minutes, Liam reappeared.

He helped her to the counter. She looked in the cardboard containers.

"We can share."

Liam took a healthy portion of the hot chicken.

"I'll sleep in your den. You'll have to shout if you need me. I did find the shower caps."

"Can you tuck me in?"

He stopped with the fork poised in the air.

"I can tuck you in. That's all. I told Hugh I was only here to take care of you until you are better. Besides, I prefer to chase my women around. You are tippy."

"I was teasing about the tucking me in."

Liam looked into her eyes. She was playing him again. The woman liked games and flirting on occasion.

"I know."

Penelope ate a piece of chicken.

"You are a nice guy."

Liam sighed.

"I might not be tomorrow."

She bent over and kissed him on the mouth.

"Thank you once more."

He didn't know if the kiss was for taking her to the hospital or for dinner

"You're welcome."

30 Blackmail Attempt

Friday Donnie watched the cloudburst. The rain hit the tin roof of the shack they were living in. There were only a thousand dollars left of the money from his first job. The roof leaked and he used stolen napkins to wipe the water.

"We need to leave this dump."

He put the note in an envelope and licked it shut. He put the killer's name on the note this time. Colleen was reading a magazine when he would go out to deliver the note. Donnie needed to take several busses to reach the man's house.

"I might be gone for three or four hours. Don't wait up."

Colleen watched him leave. He disappeared from her view on the sidewalk. The place was damp. She sneezed and coughed.

She grabbed her backpack and left. She walked in the rain and hitchhiked to reach her mother's house. She peeked in the windows. Her mother should be at work. Slowly she opened her bedroom window. The window stuck. Colleen hit the edge and shoved harder. She climbed inside.

Colleen changed into dry clothes and hung up the old ones. She laid down on her lumpy mattress for a half hour before she wandered into the kitchen. There were dishes in the dish drainer. Automatically, she put them away. Finding the large jar, she made herself a peanut butter sandwich and found an unopened bag of chips.

A container of sour cream was taken out of the refrigerator. She dunked the chips in the white mixture.

"Cold."

Putting the lid on the sour cream, she finished her sandwich.

She looked around the kitchen and saw her bracelet on the window ledge. Colleen immediately put the bracelet on and looked at the time.

The bathroom contained a bottle of cough medicine. She grabbed a spoon out of the kitchen drawer and put the items in her backpack. At the last minute, she grabbed a long sleeve fuzzy orange sweatshirt. The hanger fell to the floor. Colleen crawled back out the window. She pulled the window down and started walking to the shack. The rain stopped.

In the meantime, Donnie reached the killer's house. He peered at the house from the bushes. He watched as the killer and his woman drove away. Donnie placed the blackmail letter inside the front door. He ran to catch the bus back to the shack.

He gave the killer two weeks to get him more money. The bus stopped. Donnie placed the metal box. The box was where he said it would be found in his note. The killer should put the money inside the box and turn the lock. Donnie caught the last bus which stopped four blocks away from his place.

He went inside the shack. Colleen was chopping celery for canned bean soup. He stood next to her and noticed the medic bracelet and a different shirt.

He grabbed her hand, and she quickly dropped the large knife which rattled in the sink.

GRAY AREA FOR A WOMAN

"You lost your bracelet, and now you are wearing it again. The shirt is different. Where did you go to find your bracelet and the shirt? Answer me!"

Colleen rubbed her wrist.

"On the ledge."

"What ledge?"

"My mom. Cough medicine."

He walked away in disgust.

"I told you to never go back there. The cops are looking for us. She is the first place they will go. I take care of you. I'm going to get more money. Two weeks and we can leave this dump. I would have bought your medicine."

Colleen didn't say anything. She picked up the knife and put the celery in the cooking bean pot. She put more water on top and some salt.

"Make sure you turn the heat to low. I don't want to clean the stove again."

Colleen did as she was told.

"Low."

He got out of the chair to make sure the burner was on low.

"Okay, you found the correct spot. The burner is on low. It stinks in here of mold."

Colleen sat down on the stool and watched as he set the timer.

"When the timer buzzes, turn the knob to Off. There's a white line."

She nodded.

"I'm going to the store that has the day-old bread. Leave the window partially open. We don't want you breathing mold spores."

Colleen watched him leave. She took out two plastic bowls and plastic spoons. She dug in her backpack for the cough medicine and washed the spoon. She put the items in her backpack.

"Park sunshine is where to go tomorrow."

31 Dodge in the Park

Saturday, Dodge sat with the dog in the park. He unwrapped one of the hotdogs and threw it in the air. The dog caught the meat.

"Good dog."

He ate his hotdog and opened the bag. There were three more hotdogs left from the boys at the jail. After the volleyball game, there was a hotdog fest. They gave him a large container of coleslaw, beans, and twelve hotdogs which he put in his small apartment's refrigerator on Friday when he left the jail. The rest of the hotdogs he reheated this morning before going to the park. Dodge threw another hotdog in the air. The dog caught the meat and bun.

"Good dog."

A young girl watched him. She crept closer. Her movement triggered Dodge to be wary. The dog looked around.

"Easy. We need to be quiet."

The girl held out her hand as Donnie taught her to beg.

"I bet you like hotdogs, too. I'll give you a hotdog if you tell me your name."

The girl contemplated.

"Colleen."

Recognition hit Dodge. The girl must be Colleen Brewster. She fit the description but didn't look like her picture. He would never have pointed her out in a police lineup.

He took a hotdog out of the bag and handed it to her.

"A deal is a deal."

"Dog."

"I borrowed him from a friend. I get to take care of him a little while longer. You should see him catch hamburgers. I throw them higher."

Dodge whistled. The dog came to immediate attention. He whistled a different sound, and the dog relaxed in a sitting position.

Colleen was fascinated and slowly ate her meal.

"I have one left. I'll give you half, and we give the dog half. But you have to tell me your last name."

He took the hotdog out of the bag. The dog sat at attention and did not move.

"Deal or no?"

Colleen looked at the dog.

"Brewster."

Dodge broke the hotdog in half and gave her both pieces. She threw one half in the air, and the dog caught it.

"You have to tell him he is a good dog as a reward."

She stopped eating.

"Good dog."

"Very good. He likes you. His tail is wagging. My name is Dodge. I come to the park every day until my friend calls me. Do you live close?"

Colleen nodded.

"Which way?"

She coughed and pointed. Dodge fished a roll of hard candy out of his pocket.

GRAY AREA FOR A WOMAN

"Butterscotch sometimes cures a scratchy throat. I live twelve blocks away from this spot in that direction."

Colleen pointed to his cellphone in his pocket and the earphone with the cords.

"I like the long cords. There are new earphones that I don't trust. No cords at all."

Dodge knew she didn't understand. He motioned putting the earplugs in his ears and then her trying them on.

She nodded.

He placed them in her ears and selected a song. He gave her the phone and pointed.

"Press down and the music will play."

Colleen pressed down, and her eyes lit with pleasure. He let her listen to the song. When the music ended, she gave him back his phone and the earplugs. She didn't know there were more songs.

She held up four fingers.

Dodge put his cell phone in his pocket. He knew the music helped. Penelope told him about her reaction to sound.

"Music is the best."

"You like music and live four blocks away from here. Good. We have things in common."

"You have a deep voice. I do hear better."

He watched as Colleen put the butterscotch in her mouth. She could talk in full sentences when she wanted.

"Sweet."

She left him. Dodge slowly took out his phone and made the call to Hugh.

Hugh answered.

"You found Colleen Brewster and talked with her. Where does she live? I'll get the police to check the place."

"She lives four blocks north from where I'm sitting in the park."

"Gee, Dodge, four blocks. I have no idea where you are sitting in a large park in this city. Let me guess. No, I need an address."

"Hugh, sometimes you get on my nerves. I don't have an address yet. Tomorrow she will be back. She likes butterscotch. We'll try hamburgers for lunch."

Dodge hung up.

Hugh couldn't believe the man didn't follow Colleen. He walked over to Liam's desk.

"We need to fire Dodge. He let her walk. He found her, and she left. That's not good surveillance moves. He went to a different police school than we did. It's called the Lax School of the Century. Who does that kind of stuff?"

Liam's feet were on his desk. He came to the office first before going home. Penelope was better and told him he should go home and change. She mentioned a shave was required.

"Firing Dodge doesn't have any effect. At least he didn't scare Colleen. He was working on the friendship route. She's eighteen but not really."

"What if Donnie makes her move again? She might tell him about the old man with the spoiled dog in the park who gave her food and candy."

Liam threw his toothpick away.

183

"Relax. Tell me what Dodge said."

"He's going to try hamburgers tomorrow. He said she had a cough but looked dressed appropriately for the weather."

Liam rubbed his forehead. He didn't sleep too well the previous evening. He didn't tell Hugh that Dodge sent him an updated photo of Colleen.

"Colleen may show or not. If she doesn't, he'll go looking for her. Let him do his job."

"At least the dog is gone from my place. You should have seen my kid's faces this morning. I told them we still have the goldfish. They should be thankful. They went crying to their mom. Now I'm in trouble with Emma for not being sympathetic and hurting their feelings."

Liam screwed up his face.

"I'm out of here. Hugh, sometimes, you suck as a dad. I would buy huge rolls for breakfast and a puzzle with a dog picture at the bookstore."

Hugh watched Liam leave.

"I could buy a second goldfish. The rolls and puzzle sound better."

Hugh thought about his kid's reaction.

"Pizza with anchovies. Perfect."

Emma called and he sprung the new pizza idea on her. Hugh hung up.

"Plain pizza and plain ice cream. What's the world coming to? My kids don't like pepperoni. I was brought up on the stuff and look how great I turned out. Emma already bought rolls for breakfast. The puzzle. She didn't get the puzzle."

Hugh drove to the bookstore. The man was going to lock the door. Hugh waved his badge. The man didn't react. He put his hands together in prayer. The man let him in. Hugh found the dog puzzle and went to the counter.

"Thank you so much. My kids need this puzzle."

"Third dog puzzle we sold today. Last week the run was on birds and cats because of the cartoon shows. The poodle was the first one this morning. This one looks like a police dog," said the cashier.

"The puzzle couldn't be more perfect."

Hugh nodded to the man as he exited the bookstore.

"Peace."

He looked at his watch. Hugh started running. His watch showed eighteen minutes to get to the pizza store. The ice cream was at the grocery store which stayed open later.

32 Metal Box

That same Saturday, Donnie moved from the shack after Colleen told him about the nice man in the park with a dog that she met. He dragged her with him to a basement bedroom apartment. The only problem was no stove or refrigerator.

"At least there is no mold."

As each day passed, Donnie became more nervous about the metal box.

"I shouldn't have given the killer so long to get the money. He might have put the money in sooner."

Colleen's cough was better. The basement apartment was dryer. The walls were covered with new boards and the floor was painted. She found a small rug in a dumpster to put by their door.

Donnie checked the metal box every day.

Wednesday he left the basement and gave Colleen a sandwich to eat. She ate the turkey.

"I'll get chocolate milk on my way back."

By evening, Donnie hadn't returned. There was no food in the house. She ate her last butterscotch.

Thursday, Colleen grabbed her backpack and went to the park to find the man with the dog.

Dodge saw her and waited until she petted the dog.

"Hello, Colleen, nice seeing you again. I didn't buy any food. I thought I would wait until I saw you. We can check out the food truck and get some hamburger or tacos."

She followed him to the truck. He ordered six of the large size tacos, and they sat on the park bench eating.

"I moved."

Dodge gave the dog his last bite.

"I wondered where you went."

Colleen fidgeted with her backpack. She pointed at his phone with the headphone wires.

Dodge figured out she wanted to hear. He took his cell phone out of his pocket and found a music selection with five songs. He put the phone in her shirt pocket and put the headphones in her ears. He made sure the volume was on medium and scrolled through the artists until he found the album. He hit the start button.

Colleen's eyes grew large. She began singing.

Liam waited until the album ended. He removed the headphones and phone.

"You like music on an album."

Colleen looked wistful.

"I'm going home."

Dodge didn't want her to leave.

"Is anything wrong? I might be able to help."

"My friend is gone."

Dodge believed she meant Donnie.

"How long?"

She held up one finger.

"He's been gone a day."

Colleen frowned and looked around the park. She didn't see Donnie.

GRAY AREA FOR A WOMAN

Dodge's phone rang. Hugh told him they found Donnie dead near the beach. He fell out of a tree and hit a rock. The coroner thought the man broke his neck.

"Crazy Donnie was holding an empty metal box. We've been looking all over for him, and he shows up dead. Unbelievable bad luck."

Dodge hung up.

"Sorry. I was waiting for a call. You know I've been thinking. I miss my mom. I haven't seen her in almost a year. She lives in Colorado. I must take an airplane to get there or take the scenic route. The drive over the mountains is fun. Where's your mom live?"

"Close."

Dodge decided to take a leap of faith.

"Would you like me to walk you to your mom's place? You could wait there for your friend. The park thins out in the afternoon. You could come back tomorrow."

Colleen didn't speak. The dog put his paw on her.

"Yes."

Dodge stood up.

"Lead the way, my lady." Dodge bowed.

She giggled.

"Here, I'll let you walk the dog while I get out the cookies."

Colleen took the leash. He handed her a sugar cookie with purple-colored sugar. They went to her mom's house. She handed him the dog leash and disappeared.

Dodge stood there wondering where she went. The front door opened. She smiled and waved.

"Bye."

"Colleen. I won't be in the park anymore. My friend has returned, and he needs his dog. I'm going to Colorado."

"You will visit your mom in Colorado."

"Yes, I will. You keep safe and stay with your mom. Keep speaking in sentences and people will understand. Short words sound foreign. I like your purple tongue."

She nodded and shut the door.

Dodge walked a few steps.

"Wait a minute, please."

Dodge stopped. Colleen handed him a crumpled note.

"Find my friend. I don't know where he went. He tried to be nice."

Dodge opened the note and read.

"I have a detective friend who might help."

He walked a few blocks and called Hugh.

"Colleen is home. I didn't check her backpack nor ask her where she moved. However, there is an interesting note she gave me. The metal box might make more sense. I'll drop the note off with Kamilla at the office. The handwriting must be Donnie's. The contents of the note are interesting. Too bad, there's no name written at the start of the note. This must have been a draft."

"Thank you, Dodge. I'll read the note later after we go to the morgue."

"Tell Liam I'm leaving. I'll return the dog in two or three weeks to its owner. We're going to Colorado to fish. He can mail me my check."

"Fishing sounds fun. Make sure you fry the fish before you give it to the dog."

"Of course. He likes his cooked fish on a bun with tartar sauce."

Hugh couldn't believe it.

Dodge laughed.

"Gotcha. The dog doesn't like the tartar sauce. Too much horseradish so we use mayonnaise."

Hugh sat in the car. Penelope jumped in.

"Here's your chocolate shake."

He took the container and sipped through the straw. She waited for him to start the car.

"The spoiled dog eats fried fish with mayo."

Penelope took the lid off and used her spoon on the thick strawberry shake.

"This tastes very strawberry. I take it you talked with Dodge?"

"Colleen finally went home to her mom."

Penelope screamed with delight and hugged Hugh.

33 Friday, Eighth Week - Autopsy

Liam and Penelope came out of the briefing with their boss.

"Too bad about Donnie. We needed to talk to him regarding the burn job." Penelope's expression showed disappointment.

Liam glanced at the calendar on his phone. Donnie was dead. The man would have been safer staying in prison. Fate and bad people fixed his clock.

"After today, this will be your eighth week. I'll submit your review to the Captain. There's no need to worry. You've been an excellent partner. I know Hugh feels the same way."

Penelope was happy today was over.

"My parents have decided to check their bedroom at the condominium. They are anxious to see the place. My mom has some pictures she framed. They are visiting for the week. I'm taking Monday off. I appreciate the review update. Stay out of trouble while I'm gone."

Liam watched her leave. He went into the office and forgot his badge in the car. He went down to get the badge and saw Penelope talking with Marvin in the parking lot.

"What is he doing here?"

He watched as Penelope stepped into Marvin's car, and they drove away.

"Dinner. The man is taking her out to eat. You knew he would come back."

GRAY AREA FOR A WOMAN

He went into the office to complete his report and review of Penelope. After he was done, he sat thinking. Dodge called him.

"Liam, you should see the large trout that I'm frying. Even I'm salivating."

"Dodge, we miss you already. What type of bait did you use?"

The two men talked for twenty minutes.

"How's Penelope doing?"

Liam thought about his partner.

"Great. She's having dinner with the District Attorney, and her parents are coming here for a visit."

"Too bad about the DA. I met her father once in Montana. We were fishing in the same river and talked about his horses. He has some nice ones for trail riding. Better luck next time. You should have asked her to dinner. Women like feeling appreciated."

"You've got things wrong. I've already got a girlfriend."

Dodge flipped the fish over. Liam could hear the fish sizzle in the pan.

"You certainly fooled me."

Liam wasn't going to share any more personal information.

"The autopsy report was different than we expected."

Dodge took his fish off the fire. The dog sat watching the pan on the wooden stump.

"How different?"

"There was a snake bite on his neck. The police looked all over for the snake."

Dodge wasn't exactly surprised.

192

"There was a possible surprise in the box? The snake made Donnie fall. We're looking at murder?"

"Not sure, Donnie did break his neck before the venom took hold."

"I bet there was no money inside the box or any note. Hard to get fingerprints off a missing reptile. Know of anyone who owns a poisonous snake?"

Liam thought about a few people. The venom could identify the type of snake. He chuckled at Dodge's joke.

"I'll check around."

"The snake is probably dead by now. There is a for-hire market for snakes to eat in LA."

"I know."

Dodge hung up the phone.

Liam shook his head. He wasn't sure how he got himself into this predicament. He didn't like the fact Penelope was having a dinner date with another man. Dodge guessed why he was upset. It wasn't the case.

He drove home, and Becka was in his driveway. She moved her vehicle so he could park in his garage. They went inside his home.

"You were supposed to call me."

"I was busy. We were at the morgue today and a briefing."

"We've been dating for about fifteen months. I think we should talk about more permanent arrangements."

Becka came close to Liam and kissed him. He looked at the ceiling. She pushed away from him.

"From the look on your face, I guessed wrong."

"The timing isn't right. My day wasn't exactly a winner. We can talk about this subject some other time."

"Sure. I've made reservations on the pier at the restaurant you enjoy. I thought we could do fish tonight."

"Fish will be fine. Let me shower first to get the smell of the morgue off."

Liam disappeared to the master bedroom. Becka looked around the home. There were some changes she would make to the living room. She thought they could expand and put a porch out front to let more light into the room.

She heard the shower water stop. Becka went into the kitchen and waited.

34 Killer and Snake Bites

The killer read the note from Donnie. The person wasn't pleased. The matter would have to be taken care of soon. The note was placed on the desk. The money was available, but the person wasn't sure if this would be the last payment requested.

"We need to buy some time. I'll get the money package ready."

The killer's visitor saw the note and disappeared. The visitor knew a home-based snake dealer. The snake was smaller and easier to catch with a dead mouse.

Monday, Liam took Carter with him to the Asian and Chinese markets to ask questions about snakes sold for food. They were done with the local shops in the two areas. Some of the shop owners gave them other addresses for new shops that weren't in any directory nor had yet built their websites.

Carter and Liam walked into a tattoo shop. They were ushered in the back to talk with the owner. There were four cages. Three held snakes and one of the cages was open. Neither detective thought too much about the open cage.

The owner told them he kept records and went to his backroom to make a copy. A woman walked into the room with a live snake in her hand. They assumed she was going to put the snake in the empty cage.

Carter moved aside and undid his gun strap. Liam also moved away from the woman. He recognized the snake as a Sidewinder. The venom could range from 29 to 60 mg of venom. Forty mg could be fatal. She was closer to Carter. Carter didn't know about snakes. They all looked dangerous.

The assistant was close to the empty cage. She loosened her grip. The snake twisted and leaped out of the woman's hands as she touched the cage door.

The snake bit Carter in the leg through his canvas slacks. He yelled. Grabbing his gun, he shot the wiggling snake several times as it started to coil again. The bullets ricocheted around the room hitting Liam in the left arm, and the woman screamed from the loud gunshots.

Liam yelled, "Snake out!"

All the people in the tattoo shop went running. The front door slammed shut. The owner came into the room with his papers and looked at his assistant questioningly.

"I'm all right. They must pay for the snake. He is to blame."

The assistant pointed at Carter. The owner shoved the paper at Liam who was dialing for an ambulance and the police. Carter staggered into a chair still holding his gun.

The snake didn't move. Snakes in the other cages hissed. Carter turned his gun toward the snake cages. The assistant and the owner froze. Liam knew even a snake hiss could exude venom.

"Keep back, Carter."

"You bet."

Carter nodded before he dropped his arm and fainted. Liam grabbed a gauze bandage to put under his shirt. He couldn't remember if he yelled or not.

"Shit."

This was not the way the day was supposed to roll. The emergency people arrived first. They quickly identified the dead snake and took Carter to the hospital. A second vehicle came and took Liam to the same emergency room. Before the emergency people shut the door to the vehicle, the owner tried to hand him a bag.

"Sir, what's in the bag?"

"The dead snake."

Liam raised his head from the gurney.

"No snakes allowed in the vehicle," said the emergency vehicle technician.

Liam laid back down with relief. His boss was not going to believe him. The whole office wouldn't believe what happened. The emergency people shut the doors and drove away.

"I guess a gunshot wound is safer than a snake bite on any day of the week."

Liam felt sorry for Carter. Carter hadn't wanted to search out the snake shops. Kamilla put him on the roster.

On Tuesday, both Carter and Liam were in the Captain's office when Penelope arrived. Hugh came to talk with her.

"Why are they in the boss's office?"

"I don't know, Penelope. Let me ask Kamilla. First, I will get some scones from the bakery."

Penelope saw the delivery boy standing at her desk. He was carrying a bouquet of orange tiger lilies and green ferns. He deposited the flowers on her desk.

GRAY AREA FOR A WOMAN

She groaned. Today was not a good day. She quickly read the card.

Dinner was the best. We'll do dinner again. ME.

Hugh arrived with the scones.

"Nice bouquet. Can I take this one home to Emma? She adores lilies."

Penelope took the card off.

"Please remove the bouquet."

Hugh handed her the scone bag and moved the flowers to his desk. He returned.

"You brought in the stuffed monkey. He looks cute on your monitor. I didn't know the arms bent. Wait until my kids see your office on family visit day."

Penelope touched the monkey and looked at Hugh.

"Oh, yeah, there was a snake."

"What?" said Penelope.

"Carter got bit, and Liam got hit with a stray bullet. Fortunately, the bullet glanced across his arm and didn't lodge. Still, I bet they both felt pain."

Penelope could imagine the burn.

"Who fired the gun?"

"Carter."

Penelope stared at Hugh.

"Carter shot Liam?"

"I think it was a mistake. I heard there was a stray bullet. Although I'm not sure."

Penelope sat down. At least the flowers were missing from her desk.

"I told Liam to stay out of trouble."

Hugh ate a large bite out of the raisin scone.

"This is very tasty. The bakery must use sour cream. Impossible to do in this job. Stay out of trouble, that is."

She grabbed a peach scone and took a bite.

"I should make coffee."

Hugh jumped up and helped her find the brew he liked. He made the coffee. After pouring them fresh cups of coffee, he settled in the chair.

"This is going to take some time. You should get a hassock. They have these soft and fluffy ones. My kids have them in their rooms. Of course, the hassock is smaller."

Hugh pulled over the garbage can and turned it upside down. He put his feet on the top of the upturned can.

"Shouldn't we get to work?"

Hugh looked around the office. Most of the detectives were at their desks.

"And miss the opportunity of a lifetime to talk with Carter and Liam? Not on your life. It's not every day we have snakes wounding officers, not to mention flying bullets. I wonder what happened to the snake?"

Penelope took a sip of her coffee.

"How're your parents?"

Her eyes clouded remembering.

"Oh, oh, what happened?"

"They invited Marvin to stay in the guest bedroom for the weekend."

Hugh stopped eating his scone.

"The same bedroom Liam slept. Really? I heard the DA wears silk jammies at home."

"We have guest robes with the soap. I didn't notice. I hardly saw my father. They played golf Saturday and Sunday. Dinner was brief in the evenings."

"You had dinner with the DA three nights in a row?"

Penelope stirred more cream in her coffee.

"I wouldn't mention my dinners to Liam. He might be in a bad mood. You know, wounded arm syndrome."

Hugh smiled evilly. Then he remembered the gift of flowers.

"You should tell him about the dinners."

The door to the boss's office opened, and the two wounded detectives went to their desks. The other detectives surrounded them until they heard their version of the story. The band of department detectives dispersed.

Liam saw the flowers on Hugh's desk.

"Mental note, no tiger lilies."

He also saw the stuffed monkey on her monitor. Liam left without talking to Penelope or Hugh. His arm was in a sling. He looked frustrated.

"Wow, I expected a private story for his partners. How rude!"

"I should have tossed the flowers."

Hugh put the garbage can upright. He and Penelope went to their vehicle for the day.

"Where are we going?"

"I have someone who might have seen Duane in Mexico."

She raised her eyebrows.

"The man and his wife were on a cruise ship tour. Cancun was one of the ship's stops."

"How long was their cruise?"

"Three weeks," said Hugh.

"In other words, Duane Hicks might not be there anymore."

"I know that time has passed, and the ability to track him seems cold. However, Duane is a creature of habit. He likes staying in one place. Beverly used to say her husband bored her with his inability to have fun. Fun for her was movement."

"Why did the two of them ever marry?"

Hugh wasn't sure.

"They were an odd couple. She had her strengths, and he also did. Maybe they filled each other's gaps."

Penelope thought about the gaps in what a person said and didn't say.

"Did Liam look all right when he walked by you?"

Hugh pulled into a driveway of a stucco home in Thousand Oaks.

"Don't worry. This isn't the first time he's been shot. I imagine the snake was rattling."

Penelope looked doubtful. She didn't pick up on Hugh's humor.

"Do you want to call him?"

She looked at the black metal high fence. The edge of a swimming pool showed. She could hear the waterfall. The home was in a nice area of Los Angeles.

"No. We should complete our interview. If we don't see him, I'll call this evening."

GRAY AREA FOR A WOMAN

They went to the front door. The owners showed them the back patio where they talked about seeing Duane with a woman at a bar in Cancun.

"Was he walking around?" asked Hugh.

"Yes. He did have his arms wrapped in stretchy bandages."

"Both arms?"

The man looked at his wife and commented.

"The man drank his beer through a straw which was why we noticed him. We didn't see the newspapers until we arrived home."

"Was there anyone with him?"

The woman and man shrugged.

"Thanks, we'll be in touch if we need any further information."

Hugh escorted Penelope to their vehicle. She paused.

"Duane must have had an accident while in Mexico. I wonder if he knows Beverly is dead?"

"I was startled to hear the cruise couple's story. I'll talk with our boss. The Mexican authorities can check the bar. Duane and his friend, Dee Anne Fuller, might return some evening. We hope they do. This case has taken too long. We have some other cases coming our way."

"I'm glad we figured out Dee Anne's first and last name. Too bad her record was almost clean. She had a few speeding tickets."

Penelope received the shortened summaries of the new cases yesterday.

"Donnie's jail mate is getting out of prison. I wonder how much Donnie told him?"

"We know Donnie visited Mark Johansen the week before he died."

"We should talk to Mr. Johansen while he is in jail," recommended Penelope.

"The boss wants us to wait until the man is out."

"Why?"

"Johansen's dad is in high society. His kid belongs to the privileged. We must catch him without a lawyer around. Getting close to Mark in or out of prison is the problem."

"What did he do?"

Hugh sighed.

"He broke into a few houses. One neighbor wouldn't drop the charge which was too bad. He made a mistake. The judge parked him in jail for five years. His bad luck continued when they put Donnie with him in the jail cell."

35 After Work with Liam

Penelope sat on the warm sand. She and Hugh returned to the office earlier. She changed into her exercise outfit and tennis shoes at work. Instead of driving home to her condominium, she drove to the beach and parked near the cement breakwater. Liam wasn't picking up any phone calls. She waited until she saw the man walk past her.

She adjusted her baseball hat and pulled her ponytail through the back. Penelope jogged until she ran alongside him. He slowed to a stop. She slowed and turned around to face him.

"I called and there was no answer. I decided an in-person meeting was required. I'm sorry you were shot. You didn't stop to talk with Hugh or me at work. We were wondering what happened. I imagine your arm hurts. You should have called us from the hospital. We are your partners in case you have forgotten."

"Go home, Penelope."

Liam walked in the direction of his home. She walked alongside and didn't talk. They reached his garage, and he used the clicker to open the door. She followed him. He held his laundry room door open for her. Liam knew she wouldn't obey his command.

She sat on the stool in the kitchen. He slid a cold bottle of beer toward her and opened one for himself.

"The woman held this three-foot snake she was returning to a cage. Snakes look harmless but aren't. The head was shaped largely in the front which meant poisonous. We have them in California although

Australia has the most poisonous. The venom contains zootoxins which will immobilize prey. The snake jumped toward Carter's leg and bit him. He panicked and started shooting. I didn't blame him. He was faster getting his gun out. There wasn't any fire ax on the wall. There should have been. Anyway, a stray bullet hit my arm. I called the EMT's and the police. They arrived almost immediately which was good for Carter. The owner tried to give me the dead snake for food. The whole scene was nuts. I was embarrassed."

Penelope rubbed the beer label.

"Correction, I'm still embarrassed."

"Other than your wounds, the incident is kind of funny."

"Funny. Are you kidding? That is why I didn't stop in the office to talk with my partners. Wait a minute; I'll show you funny."

He proceeded to chase her around the kitchen island until she accidentally touched his arm when he was tickling her.

"Ouch!"

He stopped close to her. She looked at his sling with concern. Her eyes were misty, and her lips were close. Liam bent and kissed her. She kissed him back. He groaned.

She stopped.

He backed away.

"The flowers got to me today and the monkey."

Penelope saw how he connected the two items.

"Hugh bought me the monkey when I was in surgery. Are we okay, now?"

GRAY AREA FOR A WOMAN

Liam thought about his comments the first day he saw her decorated desk.

"The monkey gift is not funny. Let's call the toy a private joke between Hugh and me. I believe buying you any kind of flower scared him. I understand that stuffed toys were safer. However, I hate that the DA sends flowers. They are like a trophy or something. Even though they were sitting on Hugh's desk, I noticed the flower shop's signature card."

"I'll ask him to stop sending flowers."

Liam gritted his teeth.

"No. I'm an idiot. You can have flowers and eat out."

"Why do you get upset by Marvin?"

Liam stared at the ceiling.

"His being around the office so much since you arrived irritates me plus he makes more money."

Penelope peeled off the label and crumpled the paper.

"I should go. I needed to make sure you were feeling better. Are you better?"

He moved close.

"I could use a friendly hug."

Penelope hugged him. He wrapped his arms around her. Their bodies warmed. He enjoyed her softness too much and pulled away.

Liam touched her face.

"You are beautiful. Thank you for worrying about me. You were right. I should have talked to you at the office. Yet, if I had, you wouldn't be here giving me much needed sympathy. You made me feel better."

She smiled.

"I'm returning the favor of when I was hurt. Tender loving care among friends is a good thing. Goodnight, Liam."

"Goodnight."

She left and jogged to where she parked her car. The sun was getting lower, and soon the day would be night.

He looked at his empty driveway. The sun was setting. He looked down the street and saw her car pull into the roadway. The sky turned orange. He remembered the lilies. He was glad Hugh took them home to Emma.

Liam touched his sore arm. The ache was a thousand piercing raindrops hitting the wound. He popped more painkillers in his mouth. His arm didn't ache as much. He could feel the pills work when the pounding rain stopped. He was luckier than Carter. Carter would need to have his blood checked until they were sure the venom was gone from his body.

"This was too close."

He went into the house, took the label, and straightened the paper. The empty bottles were thrown in the trash. He found a book of poems in the living room. Turning the pages, he found the poem he wanted. The beer paper was stuck inside as a bookmarker.

The poem was about two people touching during a rainstorm.

"Watch out for the lightning."

36 Insurance Claim

The insurance agent stared at the computer screen as she read the completed form. It was Monday, and she hated the first day of the week. Each hour dragged. She scrolled the screen looking for the information.

"The man's wife died in Los Angeles. Murder is not good. Gunshot was the cause. We have a death certificate. The death certificate states the same cause and is signed by the coroner. The husband's social security number matches the file. The husband is claiming the insurance money. We have a signed insurance policy. The client has paid and is current with payments on the invoices. The address for a check shows in Cancun, Mexico. The address is valid. Check, check, check, and check."

She clicked the button.

"Approved."

The woman yawned and went on her break.

The supervisor read the form.

"All the data is complete."

He spilled his coffee and ran to get napkins. He accidentally hit the approve button when he touched the mouse clicker. The completed form disappeared from the supervisor's screen.

The manager was out for the day. His substitute approved the form from the supervisor and went to lunch.

The form went to accounting who caught the man's name. She showed the form to her manager. The accounting manager's boss was on vacation for the rest of the week. The form wouldn't be approved until he returned.

The accounting manager put a sticky note on her computer to remind her to ask the boss about the man's name. There was a red flag.

Over the weekend, the cleaning people arrived. The vacuum cleaner clogged under the woman's desk. The sticky note fell and was sucked inside the vacuum.

Monday morning, the accounting boss approved the completed form. The form went to the people who released the checks. The red flag disappeared.

The check was mailed Tuesday to a man in Mexico.

Wednesday, the accounting manager asked her boss about the completed form and the man's name. The accounting manager reviewed the closed red flag file. The boss saw the police were supposed to be notified.

"Stop the check."

"We can't, sir. The check is in the mail."

"You must stop payment on the check immediately!"

The accounting manager replied, "I can't but your boss can."

She walked out of his office. A temporary hold was placed on the check. The insurance company contacted the Los Angeles police and gave them the name and address in Mexico.

In Cancun, Duane Hicks opened his mail and saw the check for thirty million dollars. He was delighted. His partner was out shopping. He drove to the bank and went inside instead of using the drive-up window.

He gave the deposit slip and his signed check to the bank clerk. She deposited the check into his account and handed him the receipt. Duane placed the receipt in his wallet and saw the Mexican police enter the bank.

When he walked past them, two policemen blocked the exit. Duane turned around to four guns drawn and pointed at him.

"Are you Duane Hicks?"

Duane looked around. This morning he was happy. At this moment, his feelings changed for the worst.

"Is there anything wrong officer?"

The Mexican officer hated to be the bearer of bad news.

"Sir, the check won't go through the bank. The insurance company has stopped the funds on the check, and we have been called."

The bank clerk handed the reversal slip to Duane.

Duane didn't understand.

"I have to pay inheritance tax or something in Mexico first. No problem. The bank can take what they need, give the government their money, and I'll take the rest."

The Mexican officer looked at the bank clerk. She shook her head.

"How can this be happening? I had the money. Didn't I? I touched the check. There was a check. My answers are correct, but the check wasn't. I need a lawyer," said Duane.

"The police in the United States want to talk with you. There are questions about your dead wife from Los Angeles."

"No problem. I was sorry she died while I was recuperating from an accident in Mexico. We weren't exactly friendly. Everybody knows. She talked about the failure of our marriage to all the country club crowd. I can visit Los Angeles. I have air miles for a ticket. No need to arrest me."

The officer spoke.

"Perhaps you should have tried harder and brought your wife with you to Mexico with your air miles. The police have issued a warrant which we must follow."

The Mexican authorities led him away to jail and transfer to the United States. He wouldn't see his lawyer until he arrived there.

His girlfriend saw the police outside their Cancun hotel. There were too many officers with guns. She knelt and checked her funds and passport in her leg wallet. She split the area. She assumed they were taking Duane Hicks to Los Angeles for questioning.

The girlfriend made a phone call.

GRAY AREA FOR A WOMAN

37 Interview with Duane

Liam watched the outer door open. He and Hugh waited for Duane to sit down. The Captain decided the two detectives knew Beverly and Duane. They should be the ones to conduct the interview. Penelope understood. She was the new person on board.

Duane sat down.

"Liam Knight and Hugh Farris. Don't tell me! I'm here because of the two of you. I should have invited you fishing in Mexico, but my other friends came first."

"We're not here about fishing. The Los Angeles police believe you hired someone to kill your wife," said Liam.

"Are you out of your mind? We were having difficulty and talked about divorce. That is the extent of our hostilities towards each other. I don't know anyone to hire. Everyone knows me in LA. I would never get away with killing Beverly even if I wanted to which I didn't. She could have her stuff, and I could have mine. We were going to split the assets."

Hugh moved a folder back and forth.

"Did Beverly feel the same way about the assets?"

Duane looked at Hugh.

"What are you saying? She changed her mind. I don't believe you."

"The swimming pool man was a mistake," said Hugh.

Duane knew the swimming pool man wasn't in the equation.

"I was sorry to hear he was murdered at our home. Wrong place and wrong time might be a theory."

Liam watched Duane.

"How did you find out Beverly was murdered and when exactly?" asked Liam.

"I broke my arms in an accident. I tried flying over the water behind a boat on skis. I should have skipped the skiing part. The buoy got in the way. Fortunately, the life preserver stayed attached. My arms took a long time to heal. I couldn't bend my fingers until they took the casts off. I should have called Beverly, but I got busy with someone else. As soon as I could, I started trolling the internet and read my emails. A friend sent me a note about Beverly. I called and ordered her death certificate immediately. The insurance forms were online. I submitted the insurance claim the day the death certificate arrived. A normal person would do what I did. The insurance policy copy was on the laptop that I brought with me to Mexico. I always paid the insurance premium for six months in advance on both our policies."

Liam looked at Hugh. Duane was a regular, normal guy is what the man was saying. The insurance request would have been considered normal if the amount were fifty thousand dollars. Thirty million was a different story.

"You told Mason Jarett about Madeline Foster and her crew of women."

"Hugh, I told several of the boaters in Ventura about the scam she was rolling. I thought it was my duty to warn them about Madeline Foster. I didn't tell Mason."

Hugh hesitated before asking the next question. "Wasn't Dee Anne Fuller part of the scam?"

"I don't know, but she was the person who warned me via a note she slipped to me. Then I invited her to dinner as a thank you. From there, things snowballed. I went to Mexico to play. I told her where I liked to visit and stay. One day I saw her. She happened to be in Mexico staying at the same hotel. She recommended we have some fun together. I thought why not."

Liam wasn't buying the private note story. He almost bet the ski boat was Dee Anne's idea. Or Madeline's. They needed an alibi for Duane. Ideas were flowing in his brain of a massive game being played.

"Why would Dee Anne warn you?"

"I guess she liked me."

Hugh rubbed his hands over his face. Liam glanced at his partner. Hugh rolled his eyes and stood up. Liam knew women could weave a magic spell on men. He felt some when he hugged Penelope.

Liam twirled his ink pen in thought. "There is a huge sum of money that might make you more attractive without a wife in tow."

Hugh couldn't believe Liam needed to explain things to the man.

"Are you trying to warn me or scare me?" asked Duane.

Hugh undid the folder and slid the two burned body pictures and the mug shots.

"This should scare you. These two people probably murdered your wife. I'm sure you met Connie. Cougar was the man. They were found on Mason's burned boat."

Duane looked at the pictures with doubt in his eyes.

"You aren't certain they killed my wife?"

Liam handed the picture back to Hugh who produced another one.

"This guy burned the boat enough to sink it in Ventura Harbor. He didn't know two bodies were inside until he saw the news. Putting two and two together, Donnie Corwin wrote a blackmail note to the killer. Somehow the meetup with the blackmail money went awry. A snake scared the man, and he broke his neck falling out of a tree. The snake was a plant by the killer."

Duane looked at the picture.

"I never met this man, nor do I recognize the name. I thought the snakes were in the hills, not in the parks."

"Geesh, Duane, where do you think someone bought the snake," said Hugh sarcastically.

Duane ignored the detective.

"Why would this Corwin burn Mason's boat?"

"Money!" exclaimed Hugh agitatedly.

Liam knew the interview was almost over. They weren't getting anywhere.

"We believe you may be in imminent danger from the killer and the others. We suspect the women are involved and possibly Mason."

Duane looked off in the distance.

GRAY AREA FOR A WOMAN

"You're wrong. The police have no idea who killed my wife, and you are throwing people under a bus with no gas. Or should I say boat? I bet some random creep was trolling our neighborhood and picked a house. Too bad Beverly was home. I know Mason didn't take good care of his boat. Somebody did him a favor. Ask him who the two people were on his boat. Anything more gentleman? My lawyer will be with me next time."

Hugh put the second picture away.

Liam and Hugh stood up.

"You are free to go. We'll let the insurance company know we are done with our questions."

The two detectives left the room. They walked down the hall. Hugh asked Liam a question.

"Now what do we do?"

"We wait to see who makes the next move."

"The guy gets his money and walks away free. He's not even scared. Pure dumb."

Liam knew Duane would never be free. Someone had Duane exactly where they wanted him.

"Duane isn't scared yet. The money is clouding his judgment. We know he will be their next target," said Liam.

"Yeah, I guessed the answer a second after I spoke. Someone has already drawn invisible rings on his shirt for target practice. My wife said I have delayed insight."

"Our friend has no clue about the problems his future holds."

Hugh let Liam drive.

"This means our investigation is done."

Liam shook his head.

"Only this loop. There's two more to go."

Hugh sat quietly for five minutes.

"We should have brought Penelope. Her interview techniques are better. He might have listened to a woman."

Liam doubted Duane would listen to anyone.

"He is too wrapped up right now. Money does that to a person. Invincible are his thoughts."

The rolling grass and horses appeared in Hugh's sight and quickly disappeared. They were approaching the city.

"You and Penelope should come to dinner next week. Thursday night would work. The calendar on our refrigerator shows clear."

Liam smiled. The calendar was usually full of pink ribbon, colored pictures, and homemade magnets. He wondered about the change of heart.

"I thought you liked Marvin best."

Hugh grinned.

"Not so much anymore."

"What changed your mind?"

"The snake episode. You are the real deal, a true detective. Marvin only plays golf and buys flowers. His ex-wife has an extra set of keys to the Malibu house. I doubt that he's changed them."

"Gee, thanks, for the affirmation and information."

Hugh's face was contemplative. Liam grinned.

"I'll bring the steaks."

"What about wine?"

"Two bottles of red," said Liam.

"Pop for the kids?"

"How about canned lemonade? I don't want to upset Emma."

"Lemonade works."

"Seriously, Hugh, why the change? Marvin is worth millions."

Hugh figured out the change happening in the office.

"Penelope doesn't need things like other people or other women. Money is not the number one thing moving her life. She's like a breath of fresh air. You ever see a wild thing run? The wild thing is Penelope. She's tied up the boss, you, me, and Carter. She's in control. And we love her anyway."

Liam parked the car. He got the picture but wasn't going there.

"I'll break the news to Jonathan about the case. I can take the heat better."

Hugh was grateful.

"This has been the worst case. I burned the burgers on the grill last weekend. I don't ever waste meat. My neighbor called the fire department. The kids used the burned burgers for hockey pucks. I took out more of the frozen patties, and we boys had a great time grilling. Those firemen told me where to buy a sturdy ladder. They didn't like the one in my garage."

"You found some new buddies."

Hugh grinned.

"Yeah."

Liam walked past Penelope into his boss's office. The round hassock sitting at her desk was new.

The hassock looked like the ones Hugh's kids had in their rooms.

"She might as well install a wall, add stucco, and a roof."

The detective wanted to get the discussion with the boss over with.

"The scale tips either direction. We either did good or screwed up."

His only hope was the interview he had arranged with Mark Johansen for tomorrow would work. The boss needed to approve the off-the-wall and secret meeting. Liam needed a break in the case and wanted to park someone in jail. There was one person he wanted immediately.

Penelope talked briefly with Hugh. He asked her if she ever dated firemen. Penelope shook her head. He told her about his neighbor.

They went home.

GRAY AREA FOR A WOMAN

38 Mark the Jail Mate

Mark pulled his car to the curb. The shiny red car was new and a gift from his father. He saw the detective waiting in the coffee shop.

"Liam Knight, I haven't seen you for a long time. Hopefully, we'll run into each other in the future at some parties. I'm looking forward to relaxing and playing. I missed the ocean and the whole scene."

Liam passed the tall coffee to Mark.

"Cream, no sugar. Mark Johansen, glad you are out of jail."

Mark opened the small slot and took a sip.

"You want to know about Corwin."

"I do. He visited you approximately a week before his untimely demise. We think he burned a sailboat in Ventura the day he got out of prison. The job probably kept him out of trouble for a short period. He decided to return to the person who hired him. He wrote a note wanting more money."

Mark stared outside.

"This interview, I won't be in trouble, will I?"

Liam looked at his coffee.

"It depends on what went down."

Mark hated uncertainty. He looked at his car. Liam liked the car.

"Nice color. How does she drive?"

"Impressive and a real machine. You still own your sports car?"

Liam's vehicle was more expensive.

"I do."

"Corwin was odd. I didn't like the guy. In prison, you must pretend. Fake is the way to safety. I created an area of calm by doing exercises. Corwin didn't exercise but ran in place. Somewhere along the way, he trusted me. I can't go back to jail."

"I'll try to keep you safe, but we need your help."

"My father's lawyer won't agree with you."

Liam looked around the coffee shop.

"He's not here."

"Corwin told me about a sailboat that accidentally caught fire. I wasn't sure if he was making up a story. I told him that I didn't want to hear about his activities. I couldn't. Then he told me about a girl he met. He was trying to take care of her. A man owed him money. I told him to get a real job. Corwin was a jerk. He couldn't take care of himself much less a girlfriend."

"Colleen Brewster is her name. She is safe and living with her mom."

Mark appeared relieved.

"I wondered if she was safe after I heard Corwin died. A snake in a tree was unbelievable."

The two men drank their coffee. Liam was used to waiting.

"Corwin told me the man was the worst he has ever met. Having been in prison, I doubted his words."

Liam believed Corwin was right.

"I'm looking for a name."

"He didn't know the man's name, but he knew where he lived. Corwin said he followed him one night before the man's supposed accident."

Liam caught the word.

"The man's accident wasn't an accident."

"He told me this guy named Cougar beat the man with a bat on his back deck. The man didn't pay for boat repairs."

Liam perked up.

"Corwin knew Cougar?"

"He was a bad dude on the street. Most people knew about him and his gun. He did know how to fix engines. Corwin knew to stay clear. Corwin said Cougar met this woman. He wanted to warn me to not get involved with either one when I got out."

Liam said, "Connie Moore."

Mark finished his coffee.

"You know more than I realized."

Liam watched Mark.

"Why did he want to see you in prison besides warning you about Cougar and Connie?"

Mark nervously flipped the top of the coffee lid back and forth.

"He needed help writing the note to the man. Corwin didn't want to look stupid."

"You helped write a blackmail note? The police have what we believe was a first draft attempt by Donnie."

Mark disagreed with the word blackmail.

"I didn't help him write a blackmail note. I can't have the police thinking I did."

Liam needed to push the interview forward.

"You helped the man write a note."

"Corwin said the man owed him money and needed him to pay. The note was requesting money and telling the man the place where to leave it. That's all I know. If I give you an address, what happens next?"

Liam explained the process. Mark fidgeted.

"I'm worried the man who lives at the address might have his people come after me."

The detective thought about reality.

"Look, there are no guarantees in this life. You chose, or you don't. I think his people might be delighted the man is out of the picture and in jail. If we can catch him, that is."

"Can I use your ink pen?"

Liam handed over the pen. Mark wrote the address on a napkin, and that the man owed Corwin money. Corwin told the man to put the money in a metal box. He signed and dated the napkin. Mark shoved it toward Liam.

He looked at the familiar address.

"Mark, we can't thank you enough. You might want to call your attorney and let him know we talked."

Mark tossed his cup in the garbage. The lid rolled under a table. Mark retrieved the lid.

"Habit. I was on garbage detail. See you, Liam."

Liam waved. He sat at the table for five more minutes. The napkin was placed in an evidence bag for safe transport. Liam drove to the office thinking about Mason. Mason's girlfriend must have purchased the snake.

He walked past empty desks. The other detectives were gone. He walked into his boss's office and shut the door.

"We've got him. Donnie needed Mark's help to write a note. The box was to hold money."

223

GRAY AREA FOR A WOMAN

The evidence bag was handed to Jonathan. His Captain looked at the address.

"Good work. I'll call the District Attorney and the rest of our people. A live snake was delivered to Mason Jarett's address two days before Corwin's death. We should get a fast turnaround for the search warrant and arrest of Mason Jarett."

"Hugh and Penelope?"

"Wait until we have him. Go home. Take a load off. You've earned it."

"For a second, I thought Mark wouldn't come through. He asked me to guarantee his safety. He can't return to jail. I need our people to help."

Jonathan folded his hands.

"All Mr. Johansen did was give us an address which Corwin gave him and verification the man owed him money. We checked out the address. There should be no problem from our end. I'll talk to his dad. The boy might want to go on an extended vacation out of harm's way."

Liam didn't go home. He went to Dugan's place. Dugan gave him a fresh cup of hot coffee.

"You must be having a bad day," commented Dugan delightfully.

"No, it's a fantastic day. It's not raining."

"Where's your pretty detective friend?"

"I only get to work with her two days a week."

Dugan shook his head.

"Too bad."

"Tell me about it."

Liam drank his coffee and left. There was a phone call from Hugh. He called him back.

"Well?"

Liam knew Hugh could guess how the routine interview turned out.

"I went to Dugan's afterward."

Hugh did a little dance in the men's room at the gas station.

"I'll wait until tomorrow."

Liam hung up and went to the grocery store to buy thick steaks for next Thursday evening. He always enjoyed dining at Farris's house. Emma and the kids were fun to be around. Hugh would set up the crochet set for everyone to play. There would be cookies for prizes.

Once home, he put the steaks in the freezer. His home was quiet. In the evening, the news would have arrest information. Things would be chaotic tomorrow at headquarters.

Becka called and wanted to come over. He told her that he needed a quiet night alone. She would understand when the evening news came across. She was used to his moods. She left him alone.

He sat thinking about the next moves that might occur. The game wasn't over. There were two dangerous players left.

He hoped Mason's arrest would scare Duane Hicks to make some moves. Liam wasn't sure which direction the man would take.

"You think you know people, and then they change."

He thought about Penelope. She would understand the secrecy surrounding the arrest. Liam wouldn't need to explain. He was the lead investigator who made the final call on involvement.

Liam picked up his phone and put it down again. He would follow orders.

He checked his wine refrigerator to make sure the two bottles of expensive red wine were there. Both bottles were on the bottom. He didn't need to run to the store.

His phone rang. He listened to Jonathan for ten minutes. The man was in custody and behind bars. Liam let out the breath he was holding.

"I'm glad there wasn't any problem."

Liam went to his bedroom and took a shower. Putting on his robe, he felt better about the job. Tomorrow looked brighter with one criminal locked away.

He sat on his bed and hit Penelope's number.

She was putting her clothes away in the closet from the dry-cleaners and stopped to answer.

"Hi, we got him. Mason Jarett is in jail."

He could see her smile in his mind. Her voice softened when she smiled.

39 Dinner Together at Hugh's

Hugh held his wine glass high in the air.

"A toast to my beautiful wife, to Penelope's twelfth week with us, and Liam finding victory in putting one bad dude in jail."

They all toasted. The warm steaks were on a platter with twice-baked potatoes and a huge bowl of corn on the cob. Liam helped Hugh cut the steak into small pieces for the kids while Emma and Penelope sliced the potatoes and broke the corn in half.

They ate their meal. The kids looked tired from playing crochet and wrestling with Liam and Hugh. Emma's maid took the children upstairs to sleep.

Everyone helped clear the table of food and dishes into the kitchen. Hugh brought the silver pitcher of coffee, and Liam brought the tray of cups and cream.

The men talked about past assignments and things that went wrong at work. Emma and Penelope listened to their stories.

"One time we ran through a barn. The barn was empty, and we were okay until we saw the bull."

Emma knew the story. Penelope exclaimed, "Hugh, what did you do next?"

"Run the other direction, of course. By the way, Liam, thanks for your help hanging the hammock."

Liam nodded and took the silver pot in the kitchen. He refilled the container with more coffee. He walked back into the dining room and spoke.

GRAY AREA FOR A WOMAN

"The farmer with the pitchfork was taken into custody by Carter. He was charged with fraud. The sperm he was selling was from a different bull."

The maid brought in the dessert. There were cherries with ice cream. The dessert bowls were passed around.

Liam complained, "Where's the tower of wiggly stuff?"

"We ran out of the red color," said Hugh.

Emma noticed how happy Penelope was around Liam. She was different from her last visit.

"Where exactly did you live in New York City?" asked Emma.

Penelope put her fork down. She didn't want to talk about New York.

"Close to Greenwich Village."

"How much fun? I love New York. The city bustles with life."

Liam watched Penelope wrestle with her next words. He interjected.

"Not me. I prefer Los Angeles."

"Me, too," said Hugh.

Emma looked at Liam. He was protecting Penelope. She wondered why.

"Yes. The weather here is warmer, and the kids get to play outside. I forget about the cold and snow."

Liam put down his napkin.

"Emma and Hugh, this has been another wonderful meal and evening. However, we have work to do tomorrow. Penelope, are you ready?"

She stood up.

"I am ready."

She hugged Emma and Hugh.

"When my parents are here, we will go out for the evening. Thank you for dinner."

Liam helped her with her jacket. He went to his car, and he drove them to headquarters. He stepped out and walked her to her car.

"I appreciated not having to drive across town to Hugh's place."

"The evening was a pleasant one."

"The best part was seeing you and Hugh cheat playing crochet."

"We didn't cheat. We helped move the kids' balls faster because we were ravenous. Hanging the hammock took too long."

"The steaks were cooked perfectly. Well done on the bottom."

He chuckled.

"Next time, we'll do two platters. Children and an adult one."

Penelope was silent. She dug her car keys out.

Liam touched her hand. He was going to mention New York, and something held him back. He released her hand.

"Watch the potholes on the right as you exit the garage. I swear they are three times bigger than this morning."

"I will."

Liam started his car and followed her out of the parking area. He turned off the freeway on a road toward the beach. She continued North.

40 Duane's Marriage License

A month later, Hugh read the marriage license in the newspaper. He dropped the paper on the floor and called Liam. He walked around the newspaper as if the thing were contaminated.

"Duane Hicks is probably married by now to Dee Anne. Their marriage license was in last week's paper."

"Last week? Unbelievable or a smart move. He can't testify against her. We don't exactly have anyone to confirm she was going to steal his boat nor whether she participated in the forty-five-foot sailboat heist. Beth didn't know where Dee Anne was on that day and Madeline has disappeared."

"Madeline is a piece of work in my book," said Hugh.

"She also said they were acquaintances only. I beg to differ with her. They appear to be much more," said Liam.

"Our warnings to Duane didn't work."

Liam wondered what was coming next. The smart move for Duane would be to cash out the assets and hide the money. Duane wouldn't care about keeping things and would use the money. Most new wives wanted more expensive and newer everything.

"They will sell the property in Squaw Valley first. This should give us some time to work on a plan."

Hugh picked up the paper and threw the item in the trash.

"I don't have a plan. What's your plan?"

Liam didn't exactly have a plan.

"The plan is in the works."

"Don't try to fool me, Liam. There is no plan. You are at a hard stop in the case. We're screwed until Hicks is dead."

"Maybe I can talk him into faking his death."

Hugh put his slippers on and went to the door. Liam could hear him yell *Moron* to the newspaper boy.

"They always throw the paper in the bushes. I have to crawl around the bushes to find my newspaper."

Liam sighed.

"Get another paperboy."

"I did. He's the fifth one. It's a conspiracy. They train them to drop the stuff in the bushes. Ten bucks a week extra."

Liam's face screwed up into a laugh. Hugh's paranoia was showing.

"Pay them twenty bucks."

Hugh stopped talking.

"Joker. I'd rather yank the bushes out with a tractor."

"Where can you rent a tractor for twenty bucks," asked Liam.

"Call me when you have a plan."

The line went dead.

"A person can disappear with fifty million dollars. I wonder if I can get Duane to take a one-hundred-million-dollar policy out against his new wife. Wrong, Liam. Think again."

Liam paced his living room.

"Wires or wiretaps. Duane won't do it. Drones. Too noisy."

"A trust. Get Duane to put his money in a trust to save the whales or something. Great idea."

He called Hugh back.

"Well, sunshine, you are fast today. What's the plan?"

"A trust with a strange clause," said Liam.

Hugh took the bacon off the stove and shut off the burner.

"Now you are talking. I think Duane might go for the deal. We just have to find him."

"I'll call the realtor in Squaw Valley and check on airline schedules. Does Penelope know how to ski?"

Hugh poured himself a cup of coffee.

"How the heck do I know? Do they have any ski runs in Montana?"

"I have no idea. She surfs so she probably can ski. We might not have to ski. All she needs is a ski jacket and pants."

Liam called his lawyer to ask him about a trust document.

41 Squaw Valley

Penelope and Liam flew to Squaw Valley to meet at the realtor's office. They were going to tour the ski chalet that Duane Hicks owned under pretenses. Duane and Penelope knew Dee Anne wouldn't be around in the morning. She was at a hair appointment. The realtor agreed to let Duane show them the property.

The realtor unlocked the door. Liam excused himself to the bathroom. The realtor left Penelope with Duane.

'New ski outfit?"

"Yes, my old one is at the cleaners."

They went into the kitchen. Duane was showing her the stove when Liam entered the room.

"Liam, how did you get here and in my house? We have automatic door locks."

"My apologies for the fake interest in your property. We're not married. We needed to talk with you. This is my other partner, Detective Penelope King. Can we sit down?"

"Hello, Ms. King. Of course, we can sit at the kitchen table. My wife will be back in a couple of hours."

"We know. Your realtor mentioned her appointment," said Penelope.

Liam took out the papers his lawyer prepared.

"We saw your marriage license in the newspaper and became extremely worried. Next, we saw this property go up for sale. We believe once this property is sold, your life will be terminated due to the thirty million and potential for over twenty-five-million dollars that could be inherited immediately by your new wife."

Duane thought about what Liam told him.

"The way you said terminated scares me."

Penelope took over.

"In the beginning, love is sweet and hopefully kind. We think a trust document might ensure your safety."

Liam handed Duane the documents. He read through them.

"We think you should sign right away, show your wife the copy, and we keep a copy. I would not let anyone else know about the document. Your lawyer is included in the exclusion. He won't get a copy. This way, we have a controlled environment to work."

"You don't trust my wife?"

Liam looked at his friend.

"There are killers out there. We want to force them away from you or out in the open."

"My money is put in a trust for her. If I die, she can't access the money for five years. During the five years, if she commits a crime and is arrested, the trust goes to save the California wetlands. I could sign the trust and change it tomorrow after you leave."

Penelope handed Duane an ink pen.

"We hope you won't. I would hate to come to your funeral."

"What about a notary?"

"I've been notarized," said Liam.

"Can I think about this first?"

Penelope looked at her watch.

"Ten minutes and we have to be gone. I got pinged your wife skipped the frost color."

Duane reread the document. He signed both copies. Liam notarized them.

"After I show my wife the document in a positive way, of course, what do I do next? I know how to spin things, but I'm not sure if she will trust me anymore."

Liam put their copy away.

"We believe she will want to return to Los Angeles. From there, we can track her movements to see if she meets anyone. We'll take care of all the possibilities."

Duane thought about the problem he was potentially facing.

"Madeline might appear."

"Yes, we hope your new wife is not guilty. We don't know for sure. Either way, you need to know the truth."

"I do. Madeline or my wife might kidnap me."

"We don't think they will. Hiding someone might not be worth the expense."

Duane rubbed his throat.

"I'll try not to screw up."

Liam and Penelope drove to the airport. Once they were settled in the airplane, she spoke.

"I think the department is taking a huge leap of faith that Duane Hicks is innocent. He could be the guilty one. In which case, we have blown our plan."

Liam talked with Jonathan extensively before the trip.

GRAY AREA FOR A WOMAN

"We've thought about him as a suspect. If he is the one, we have let him know our plans. He'll try to run. We'll be watching, and he knows we won't ever quit."

"The loops are getting tighter," said Penelope.

She looked at Liam who appeared calm. There was a part of the plan he hadn't shared with her.

"We aren't using my house. There are too many roads and harbors to disappear. When we get back, I'm moving in with you to your condominium. Duane knows where I live, and I briefly mentioned your location."

Penelope opened her mouth and shut it again.

Liam closed his eyes and took a nap. She kept running the conversation over in her mind.

Finally, the fasten seatbelt light came on, and the sound made a tone. Liam awoke. The airplane landed. They walked and rode the escalators to the parking garage. She put her things in his car.

When they reached her place, she was nervous.

"I'm glad we rode together. Was staying here a last-minute thing or part of the plan?"

Liam put his luggage in the den.

"It was Jonathan's idea. He was worried about losing people, especially our suspects."

She glanced at Liam.

"Hugh could care less where you spend the night. He's decided that I'm more likable than the DA."

Liam looked in her refrigerator.

"I'm hungry. I can make us a quick egg sandwich. Any hot sauce in here?"

She pointed at the red bottle.

He grabbed a frypan and started cooking. Penelope took her suitcase to her room and unpacked. He called her name.

There were two plates of steaming omelet with toast.

"I changed my mind about making a sandwich."

They ate their late dinner in quiet.

"We seem to always be living together."

Liam knew they weren't living together. Living together meant sex.

"There are clean sheets in the den closet. I'm going to bed."

He put their plates in the dishwasher.

"I'll clean the kitchen in the morning."

She went into her room and closed the door. Liam took a quick shower and crawled into bed. After an hour, he was still wide awake.

There was a knock on his door.

"Come in."

Penelope slid next to him under the covers.

"Could you hold me for ten minutes? I'm not feeling okay. The pressure is mounting too fast."

"Sure, come here. I should have told you sooner about the location change."

Penelope slid closer.

"Better?"

She nodded. He watched her in the moonlight fall sound asleep.

In the morning, she awoke to the smell of sausage frying. She looked around at the unfamiliar room.

GRAY AREA FOR A WOMAN

Scrambling out of bed, she halted on her way to her bedroom.

"You fell asleep. Did you know you snore? I hope you like pancakes."

He handed her a glass of orange juice.

"Fuzzy pajamas. Mental note, the woman likes warmth."

"Very funny. Yes, I like pancakes. Two, please."

"Two pancakes with sausage coming up. You have a minute to go to the bathroom."

42 Dodge and the Bird

Hugh heard a helicopter fly close to his house on Saturday. The wife and kids were out shopping. He went out to his large, fenced back yard. His phone rang.

"Dodge, is that you?"

"Hugh, I think I can land in your backyard. I need you to go sit on your porch for a couple of minutes.

"No, don't land."

The fire department would surely arrive. Hugh saw the helicopter coming down. He ran for the safety of his back porch.

The helicopter settled in his grass, a door opened, and a dog came bounding out. The dog found his favorite spot and peed. Hugh waited for the blades to stop.

"My neighbors are going to be upset. First, I burned the burgers, and now a helicopter lands in my yard."

"Don't worry. I called the boys at the fire department. They are cool. Why does your neighbor call them so much?"

"Payback for my Christmas lights. My neighbor hates my lights because the paint has peeled off. He says they are old and thinks I'm going to start a fire. The wind blows his way most of the time. However, good to see you again."

Dodge handed him a card.

"If you ever need a ride, call me."

"What's with the dog?"

"He had to go potty."

Hugh watched as the dog sniffed around his yard.

"I wanted to show someone my bird. I flew over Liam's house, and it was dark."

"Liam is staying with Penelope. There's been a new development in the case we are working on. They are on a stakeout together.

Dodge looked skyward.

"There's hope after all."

Hugh motioned him inside. He brought out the huge ham with bone.

"How many slices?"

"About ten."

Hugh carved the ham and buttered the buns. He made a tray of sandwiches, put the lettuce on the side with a jar of mayonnaise and mustard. Hugh slathered mustard on his bun while Dodge used the mayo.

"Per Liam, they are holding their own in separate bedrooms."

"Liam? No way, unless he's changed," said Dodge.

Hugh found plates for the four filled buns for Dodge. He put two buns on his plate. The dog perked up and sat quietly for his master.

Dodge broke off a quarter sandwich and threw the piece in the air. The dog caught the bite.

"Good dog."

"What new development?"

Hugh told him what transpired with their case. Dodge contemplated the news and handed the dog the rest of the sandwich.

"There is trouble. You don't know who is in charge."

Hugh finished his second sandwich. He poured two glasses of water out of the refrigerator and found the metal bowl for the dog. He filled the bowl with water. The dog drank as the two men talked.

"We need to take off before your neighbors call the police."

Hugh wrapped the rest of the sandwiches in plastic wrap and put them in a bag. He handed the bag to Dodge.

"I have no ideas to offer. I think I've been out of the force too long. All I can say is to watch yourself. Greed is a terrible thing that destroys people."

Hugh stood by as the dog and man boarded the helicopter and took off. His landline phone rang. He ignored the call.

"I should buy new lights this year or get a professional to hang them. Blow the neighbors away big time."

Hugh put the ham away and put the card with his badge.

"You never know when a helicopter might come in handy."

He thought about Liam and Penelope.

"I bet they don't know Dodge owns a helicopter."

His wife and the kids burst through the door. Emma looked at him questionably.

"Dodge showed up in a bird."

"Ah, yes, hence the comment from our neighbor that he hates our Christmas lights. I understand."

Hugh smiled.

"We'll hire someone to do the lights this year. Instead of the multi-color, I'm thinking more sophisticated."

"Sophisticated is not you. Since when did my husband not like multi-color," asked Emma.

"The chocolate palm tree Penelope received from the DA was a moment. There were tiny lights. Here, I'll show you."

Hugh steered her out to the garage and touched the button. Tiny twinkle lights lit over his workbench. The lights reminded me of you."

Emma was doubtful.

"I promise they will be bigger and more beautiful."

"I'm glad Dodge visited, but I'm wondering. Is there any ham left?"

"Enough for tomorrow," said Hugh.

Their youngest daughter came down and told them the toothpaste was empty.

"I'll get the extra toothpaste. You lock the house. We can talk about Dodge, and you can tell me what he's been up to lately."

Hugh was left alone in his kitchen. He began turning out the lights.

He went into his den and ordered new clear lights that would surround the perimeter of his house and a few extra clear bulbs.

"No more mismatched multi-colored lights. We're having large lights outside like what they put in the palm trees."

Satisfied, he went to bed. His wife was already sleeping.

Hugh turned out the bedroom lights.

"Today has been exciting. The firemen nor the police showed."

43 Another Week – Readying Stakeout

Penelope looked at her calendar. She had been in LA for eighteen weeks. Five days passed since Duane Hicks signed the trust document. It was Friday, and she was ready to go home.

Liam joined her.

"I'm thinking we should try an expensive dinner somewhere. You and I have cooked enough."

Penelope didn't want to eat in a fancy restaurant.

"How about the chicken place?"

He was in total agreement. They drove to her condominium with a bucket of chicken, mashed potatoes, and gravy. She handed him a cheese biscuit on their way home.

"I'm feeling like an old married couple," said Penelope.

Liam shook his head. He wondered why women thought about marriage all the time. Men didn't.

"Becka is driving me crazy with phone calls. She wanted to know why I wasn't holed up with Hugh instead of you."

"She doesn't understand we are on a case?"

"I've tried a dozen times."

Liam looked over at her.

"I picked up some more guns and ammo from work. The Captain insisted. We'll plant them around the condominium."

Penelope knew the police believed one of the two women would find them. They held the other copy of the trust document. They knew Duane's copy would be destroyed first without his knowledge.

"Do you think this will work? I'm getting strange prickly vibrations. We're missing something."

Liam saw the phone number on his phone. He picked up and listened. He pulled into the condominium garage.

"Let's go eat first."

Penelope put the plates on the table with napkins and forks. They ate in silence. Each person was keeping their thoughts to themselves. She put the leftover chicken and potatoes with gravy in the refrigerator. Liam put items in the garbage and took out the trash.

He returned and sat down. She brought them hot steaming cups of coffee.

"Duane and Dee Anne have traveled to LA. They are staying at his house."

Penelope knew it was only a matter of time before someone arrived at her door. Liam also knew they better be prepared.

"I want you to let me handle whoever appears. You stay behind me. I know we have bulletproof vests."

She understood.

"We'll cover each other."

Liam felt edgy. He didn't want to turn in for the evening.

"I sort of liked you when we first met. Later we went surfing, and you taught me lessons. Afterward, I liked you more."

Penelope remembered the surfing lessons.

"You kept falling over but jumped onto the board again and again."

"It's called persistence. I hate not winning."

She drank her coffee.

"Dodge bought a helicopter."

"Really. He doesn't like traffic in the city, so I'm not surprised about the bird," mentioned Penelope.

Liam smiled.

"Less smog higher up. He landed in Hugh's backyard when the kids and Emma were out."

Penelope could imagine the picture.

Liam wanted to continue talking but he could see Penelope was extraordinarily quiet this evening.

"What's wrong?"

"The enemy has the advantage. Our position isn't particularly good."

"This isn't like New York City," said Liam.

The minute he mentioned the city, he wished he could retract his words.

"You know about Allan? How long have you known?"

Liam sat on the floor with his back resting on the couch.

"Dodge mentioned something in passing. I decided to do some research. I'm sorry about your partner getting killed."

Penelope was at a loss for words.

"Does anyone else know?"

"Not that I'm aware of other than the Captain."

Penelope knew Jonathan as her boss was informed.

"I'm turning in."

Liam hit his fist against his forehead several times and talked to himself.

"Perfect timing to screw up an evening. You had to go there and mention the guy."

He didn't tell her he knew about the engagement.

Hugh called him.

"I heard the news about Duane being in Los Angeles. Things are going to crack wide open. I can feel the electricity. My cell phone won't leave my side. Or I could come down tomorrow?"

Liam didn't want Hugh to get in the crossfire.

"We can handle things."

"Darn it, Liam, I'm trying to help."

"I know. The Captain assigned us instead."

"How's Penelope handling the wait?" asked Hugh.

Liam thought about the last five days.

"We're working together simply fine. A few blips but nothing major. She went to her room."

"What about the guns?"

"Hugh, we have them neatly stored away."

"I would have hauled a cannon into the condo. I know a guy with a huge crane."

Liam couldn't help but grin.

"Or hand grenades."

"Yeah, grenades are better."

"Goodnight, Hugh."

Hugh kept talking and Liam hung up the phone on him.

"The man never stops. He must drive Emma crazy."

GRAY AREA FOR A WOMAN

Liam stood and looked at the master bedroom. He wanted to apologize for bringing up New York. He went to her door and almost knocked. He couldn't. Some things were too personal. Allan Duran was her fiancé for a month before he died.

A call came in from Becka. Liam went into the den and his current bedroom to talk with his girlfriend.

"Becka, stop. I'm on assignment. We've talked about my job in the past. I do dangerous work only when things fall apart. There will be a partner with me, and the police standing at the ready. As soon as I can, I'll be back home. No, you can't come here. We don't know who will show their faces, or when they might appear. These are bad people who kill. Stay away."

Becka argued with him. Liam didn't need the headache.

"Stop, enough. I'll call every morning and night."

Liam hated the fighting. His focus and attention must be on what was coming. He looked out the patio door and made sure the lock was turned.

44 Saturday Exercise - Madeline

Liam left Penelope a note that he was in the exercise room on the first floor and would be gone for an hour. She looked at the time on his note and the clock. She checked his room. Liam forgot his vest. He would be gone another forty-five minutes. She threw the note away.

She didn't feel like coffee this morning. Unlocking the patio door, she stepped out and smelled the ocean. Penelope went inside. At least she found some blue jeans and a clean navy cotton shirt. The vest was taken into her closet. Her wardrobe was too limited, and her laundry basket was full.

"I need more everyday types of clothes, especially knit short-sleeved sweatshirts."

Penelope left the vest. Heating a cup of water in the microwave, she opened the teabag. The timer beeped and she dunked the bag in the water.

Sitting on the couch, she remembered the vest. She looked at the partially open patio door. Penelope thought she closed the door. Suddenly, she stood up and looked around.

"Don't move!"

She turned and saw Madeline with a gun in her hand. The barrel was pointed at her heart.

"Caught you unawares, no bulletproof vest. What a shame? I want your copy of Hicks's trust document."

"Hello, Madeline, you must have gotten up early this morning. I don't know how you were able to reach my place. We're three floors high. I'm assuming you did so via my neighbors. They trust people too much and open their doors."

"Where is the document?"

She wished Liam hadn't gone exercising this morning.

"The paper is inside my black computer bag in the master bedroom."

"Which way?"

Penelope pointed. Madeline motioned with the gun. Penelope went into the bedroom and showed her the bag sitting on her dresser.

"Open the bag slowly."

Penelope unzippered the compartment and withdrew the trust papers. She handed the papers to Madeline. The woman glanced at the signatures.

"This is the only other copy."

Penelope wondered about the other one.

"Is Duane all right? I assume he told Dee Anne about his copy and this copy."

"Duane is a sap. He tells Dee Anne everything. She runs him."

Penelope glanced at her watch. She edged toward the drawer where a gun was stored.

"You don't move until I say you can move. We go back to the living room."

"My neighbors?"

"They're tied up in their bathroom. I told them I would kill you if they made a sound. They assured me they would be quiet."

Penelope sighed. The neighbors were elderly like her parents. She would have to apologize when this was over.

"Why are you doing this? The charge for stealing the sailboat would have meant eight to ten years in prison. The time might have been less. You could learn some skills, become a working member of society, and be free."

Madeline looked around.

"The princess speaks. Prison is too restrictive. All the monitoring drove me crazy. I can't do prison. You're the one trapped in your apartment with a gunman. Your furniture is nice. I want this stuff."

Madeline waved her hand around Penelope's condominium.

"I intend to own this type of condominium and much more. You and your detective friend tried to steal the money from us with your clever document. We all worked hard to get where we are."

"I assume a person in your statement includes a man by the name of Mason."

Madeline wouldn't give her any information on Mason.

"Don't be clever. Where is the other detective, by the way? The realtor told us there were two of you."

"He went home."

"You're lying. His car is in the garage. The security guard told me. He was sociable when I told him I knew your neighbors."

Penelope thought about the prior evening.

"I don't know. We fought. Liam Knight does his own thing."

GRAY AREA FOR A WOMAN

Madeline lowered the gun slightly. She motioned Penelope to stand away from the patio door.

"Look, I'm not jumping off the patio. I'll take my chances with the gun. You were brave to jump across the two patios. The drop, if you missed it, could have been the end of your life. I thought Dee Anne loved Duane," said Penelope.

"I'm used to scrambling around a sailboat and boat docks. The patios were easy. If you believe Dee Anne loved Duane, you are very wrong. Men aren't the best thing for her. We are closer. We've known each other for years."

Penelope figured out what might have happened.

"You've already killed Duane in LA."

The accusation didn't faze Madeline. "Like I should tell you."

"He doesn't deserve death."

Madeline was thoughtful.

"Deserve is a good word. Death might be a reward. I should be rewarded. He didn't come to LA. I dressed like him, used his ID, and ticket. We were going to put him in the freezer. However, the freezer is broken. Bad timing. He's in the wine room with his hands tied until we can torch the chalet. The guy has all these automatic locks. The installers messed up. We can't get the wine door open again. The door is thick is the only reason he's still alive. A new lock for the wine cooler was supposed to arrive next week."

Penelope knew she should try to take Madeline down. She looked at the patio drapery rod.

"We imagine the new owners have insurance. Don't worry, Dee Anne isn't there right now. She's at a safe distance until I call."

"The ski chalet sold. I didn't know," fibbed Penelope.

"Five million cash deal was a bonus for us."

"I'll bet."

Penelope was too far away from the gun in the kitchen drawer. She remembered arguing with Liam about putting the gun under a cushion on the couch.

"I was right."

Madeline looked at her strangely.

"Right about what?"

"The plan for a trust document wouldn't work. I was against the idea from the beginning. But no, men think they are right, and females are wrong. I hate when they do that righteous stuff."

Madeline's brow wrinkled.

"You are trying to mess with me. I don't do the men are stronger and the poor-me route."

Penelope underestimated Madeline. The curtain rod was looking more promising as a weapon. She thought about the fire alarm in the outside hallway. She wondered if she could get Madeline in the outer hallway. She figured Madeline saw the security cameras. There were matches to light candles. Lit candles would take too long to make hot wax.

"You know what? I'm tired of being a detective. Today isn't going too well. The pay sucks. I bought the cheap drapes and shouldn't have."

Now Madeline laughed.

"You are full of it. The rug alone in here probably cost two thousand dollars."

Penelope bent and touched the rug.

"This rug is from my parent's second cabin on their ranch in Montana. Trust me, this rug costs over five grand."

Madeline backed up so she could see the full impact of the rug on the floor.

"Your parents own a ranch in Montana?"

Penelope looked at her watch. The time was exactly an hour.

"Can you point the gun in a different direction? I'm feeling panic about the barrel. The thing might go off when you least expect it. You know, like lightning hitting in a storm."

"Girl, you are one weird chick."

Liam snuck into the kitchen. He was glad they installed a quiet keyless lock. He heard Madeline talking with Penelope about the insurance money. No one knew he was there. He took the revolver out of the drawer and made sure it was loaded. He put the extra bullets in his pocket. He peered around the corner and saw the two women facing each other.

The gun was pointed at Penelope's heart. He wondered why she wasn't wearing her vest. Liam wasn't wearing his vest because he went to the gym. He texted Hugh.

"Madeline is here with a gun aimed at Penelope. I'm assessing the situation. No vests. Call the calvary."

He listened.

"I'll make sure the bullet hits a vital organ. Your death will be swift."

Penelope swallowed.

She looked around the room for an object to throw. Throwing was easier than pulling a curtain rod out of a wall. She wasn't going down without a fight.

Her mother sent her an antique wooden bowl that sat on the coffee table. There were vanilla-scented candles in the bowl. She doubted there was enough time to hurl the bowl at her captor.

"Why do you want to kill me? I haven't hurt you on purpose. I only went along with the trust idea and did my job."

Madeline wavered.

"You know too much. That's why we are going to kill Duane. He isn't trustworthy either. We thought about sharing the money but threw the idea away. We want all the money from the insurance. You should have quit your job last week."

Penelope was thoughtful.

"I should have turned in my badge sooner. Montana is sounding good except Hawaii or Australia has better surfing."

Liam couldn't believe what the woman admitted regarding the insurance. They were going to kill Duane and Penelope. He didn't know if Dee Anne was on the premises. He hoped not.

Liam peeked around the corner, and Penelope saw him out of the corner of her eye.

Her breathing improved and the adrenaline started kicking into overdrive. She used her head to think of a better plan.

"My mother and father would hate to come to my funeral. They gave me this beautiful handmade bowl. I think the wood is pine."

Madeline turned her attention to look at the wooden bowl. She was going to speak.

Liam took the opportunity to come around the corner and fire his weapon as Penelope fell to the right out of harm's way. Liam entered the living room and kicked the gun away from Madeline.

Penelope crawled out from the curtains.

"I was going to use the curtain rod. I remembered the bolts the installers used. What took you so long? Is she dead?"

He bent down and checked.

"Yes. I aimed for the throat. The woman is gone."

Penelope rushed into his arms.

"She was going to kill me and Duane."

"I heard."

The rug could be cleaned of Madeline's blood. The drapes would need replacing. Liam held Penelope in his arms while the police and swat team arrived. They entered the condominium and took over.

He let her go to tell them to find Duane Hicks who was locked in his wine cellar. Liam told them Dee Anne wasn't at the ski chalet but was possibly at Hicks's house. She was probably going to run from the area when Madeline didn't call.

They walked outside and were astounded to see Hugh with Dodge and his dog.

"We can give you a helicopter ride to LA. You might want to stay at Liam's place tonight."

Penelope hugged Dodge.

"Hey, Penelope, you get to sit in the front. We'll put Liam and the dog in the back."

Liam took Penelope's arm.

"The dog sits in the front."

Dodge flew Liam and Penelope after they gave their statements to the police.

Hugh looked at the death scene. He was glad the case was almost over. There was an arrest warrant out for Dee Anne Hicks.

"Nice drapes."

Hugh wandered around the condominium. He saw the antler bowl and candlesticks.

"Works of art are appreciated. I'll have something to talk about when I see Wendy and Warren."

The police found the elderly couple in their condominium.

"If the police are here, our neighbor is okay?"

The officer nodded.

"Detective Penelope King and Detective Liam Knight are safe."

"Thank goodness. We like her parents and her very much. Liam appears to be a nice young man. This was exciting. We did hear a shot. Our bridge partners will enjoy a new story."

"Yes, ma'am."

45 Aftermath From Case

In the morning. Liam checked his refrigerator. There were six eggs left, some breakfast sausage, bread, and milk. The new plant on his counter looked promising. Cutting a couple of sage leaves, he quickly made a bread pudding type of quiche with grated parmesan cheese on top.

Penelope came down in one of his white t-shirts and sat on a stool. Her hair was mussed and standing on end. She looked a perfect mess.

Liam noted she wore no makeup. Her normal composed businesslike attire was missing. He poured her an orange juice in a large glass.

"Vitamin C works in the aftermath."

"I need to apologize for screaming in the night. I don't usually go berserk. I'm embarrassed."

Liam went to her room when he heard the scream.

"We both went through a stakeout that was hard. I get nightmares."

Penelope couldn't tell him the nightmares weren't the current case. She was glad he didn't mention any names. He assumed Madeline was to blame. She knew better.

"We can talk after breakfast. I'm good at listening. I have my own stories I could add. What is scary during the night pales."

Penelope didn't believe him. There was nothing pale regarding a prior stakeout in New York. Everything was in vivid color.

"Something smells good."

Liam felt he missed something in their conversation. He glanced at her bare legs. He wondered what was on her body besides his shirt. He could guess. The t-shirt wasn't fuzzy.

"Did you sleep all right after I came into your room?"

"I did, in spite, of Madeline Foster. I tried to distract her during the stakeout. She wouldn't bite."

"You didn't follow my instructions. I told you to wear your vest."

"Your vest wasn't exactly on your body either," mentioned Penelope.

"Yes, but I found the closest gun. I know we should have stuck a gun in the couch cushion. Next time, we will. The carpet people will remove the rug and have it cleaned. The drapes are toast. They said two weeks for cleaning because the rug needs special care."

He cut her a square slice of the egg breakfast and did the same for himself. She frowned at the square in front of her. Liam gave her his answer.

"New recipe. The name is a little of this and a little of that."

They both ate. Penelope liked the flavor.

"Unusual, but the egg, sausage, and fresh sage came through."

Suddenly, Becka appeared in the kitchen. Liam looked at his girlfriend and shook his head.

"Well, I seem to have missed the cozy breakfast party. I'm Becka, Liam's girlfriend. You must be his partner, Penelope King, with whom he sleeps when I'm not around."

GRAY AREA FOR A WOMAN

Penelope put down her fork and jumped off the stool. She remembered when Marvin's wife interrupted a pool date. This time she would be braver and leave sooner.

"Hello. People seem to get up earlier and earlier. I borrowed a shirt from his closet shelf. The shirt doesn't fit properly. We were involved in a working case. The case is over. I think I'm going to check out. I'll leave the shirt. Thanks for the egg breakfast."

Becka sat down and glared at Liam.

Within minutes, Penelope was walking out the door. He followed her outside.

"Penelope, wait, where are you going?"

"Marvin is picking me up. He is in the area because of the results of our case. I'll walk to the end of the corner. He's familiar with the cross streets. Oh, give her a piece of the breakfast thing and the recipe. I'm sure she knows how to cook."

Liam was mad when he went back into his home.

"Since when do you come here and insult a guest of mine?"

"A guest? Is that the best you can do? She was wearing your clothes. No, correction. She was wearing one piece."

Liam took the dishes off the island and put them in the sink. He didn't offer her breakfast.

"We are finished, Becka. Nothing was happening during the stakeout or afterward. You tried to make something bad, and it's wrong. Her condominium contained a dead body with blood. Her clothes contained some splatter not to mention the rug and drapes. The gunman could have killed her. I intervened which is my job. The police took over the area. She didn't have time to grab clothes. Hence, my clean t-shirt was required."

"Bullshit."

Liam raised his hand to object. He could understand his girlfriend being upset.

"She looks terrible in your shirt. You don't understand women, and how they can be sneaky."

Liam remembered Penelope's scream in the night. Both he and his partner needed calm.

"I'm her partner, and that is all."

Becka held her head high and walked out of his house.

"I hate you."

"Welcome to the club."

Liam was relieved their relationship was over. He doubted Becka would return. As a couple, they weren't working. No amount of talk was going to straighten things out. There was no reason to apologize again for doing his job.

"There go the Greece vacations."

He knew Penelope called the District Attorney. He was the last person he wanted Penelope to deal with today. The entire scene was unbelievably bad.

"Why is Marvin always in the area? The man has some sixth sense."

He thought about Penelope.

"She looked great in my shirt, particularly in the morning light."

Liam put the rest of the egg dish down the drain. Eating the egg mixture would remind him of a bad day. He got dressed and went into the headquarters' office.

His boss informed him that Duane wanted a meeting to thank him and Hugh.

"No, no, we'd like Carter to sit in for us. He can handle a thank you to the office. He might want to meet Duane Hicks."

The boss told him that Carter was on vacation.

"I figured he would take the day off."

Liam knew he wouldn't dare ask for a day off.

46 Duane's Thank You

Hugh shuffled his feet. Liam glanced around the small conference room. The meeting was delayed a day. It was Tuesday, and Penelope worked with Carter instead.

Liam sat down.

"I know Duane is late. We'll give him another thirty minutes."

Hugh strolled over to the side table and took another donut.

"These are good. Where did Kamilla find them?"

"There's a new bakery that opened. I have no idea what street they are on."

"I'll ask her later."

Duane rushed into the room with a red-headed female in a business suit in tow.

"Gentlemen, you saved me. I am thankful. I couldn't believe Dee Anne and that other horrid woman were working together. They put me in my wine cellar. The locks froze. I couldn't get out, but they couldn't get back inside. They wanted to kill me. They told me the place was going to go up in smoke. Dee Anne said I would be toast. My new wife hated me that much. I thought I was going to die, and then the rescue people arrived. My lawyer is annulling our marriage. She can't have my money or my name."

Liam watched the businesswoman.

Hugh said, "Who is your new agent?"

GRAY AREA FOR A WOMAN

Duane turned. His exaggerated fear turned to excitement.

"She is my Russian loveliness. She came to my rescue. I now see her. We found each other in the storm."

Liam remembered the voice.

"Yes, you are the woman the police called when we were on the speakerphone. You are Duane's assistant. Nice meeting you."

Hugh grabbed another donut. The raspberry jelly oozed out. He tried to lick the filling. More oozed out.

Duane bowed his head.

"Without my two friends, my life would have been over. The document idea was perfect. Tell Ms. King, she swayed me to sign. I hope she's okay?"

"Ms. King is safe."

Duane looked relieved.

"The evil woman appeared at the place you were staying. I'm glad Liam shot her. I won't be a fool anymore. Dee Anne was a horrible person. But life goes on. I leave you today a happy man. This woman is my one and only. My attorney has sent thank you notes to your boss and the District Attorney. I know he is a frequent visitor here. However, I have a plane to catch. We're flying to Seattle to check on a powerboat. Cruising the area might be a blast. I hope the boat won't be too expensive."

Hugh sat down with two napkins and a glass of water. He dabbed the napkin in the glass and rubbed it on his shirt.

"Really, where are you going Duane? The waterways are fairly large."

"I don't know. The direction South first seemed like a good idea. We'll travel as far as Tacoma. I need to get out of my Los Angeles house. It's depressing inside, and the house is now for sale. I keep seeing my first dead wife in the rooms. Oh, the buyers backed out of the Squaw Valley chalet when their realtor told them about Dee Anne."

The two detectives watched as Duane and his new friend disappeared.

"Tough luck," said Liam.

"I think I'm going to throw up. Now he's worried about his money, and how much a powerboat costs. Let me understand. Doesn't he still have lots of money for the next woman? Did you even hear a Russian accent?"

There was no sympathy in Hugh. Skepticism was in the forefront always.

"Yes, he is rich. They do have large powerboats in Seattle. The only problem is where to dock. I guess they could always drop anchor. Maybe her ancestors came from Russia."

Hugh missed the sarcasm.

"What is that expression about a fool?"

Liam rolled his head. His shoulders were stiff.

"Money wasted or gone mad or stupid. I can't remember."

Hugh never liked Duane.

"He's a schmuck. Stupid of the highest order. Dee Anne is still out there and not a happy camper. I'm going home. It's safer there. My house is on a solid foundation and doesn't rock. The fire department and cops have my address. I don't even have to call them."

Hugh put the napkins in the garbage and left the room. Liam sat in the conference room.

"A wasted day and a few nights. Another relationship in the toilet. I'm going home. Hugh's right. Wait a minute."

He opened the door and yelled. Hugh turned.

"When Dee Anne finds out that Duane has a new chick in the coup, we have a new situation on our hands."

Hugh walked toward the detective. He rubbed his hands together.

"Oh, goodie. I was hoping you picked up on my words. A hen fight, how interesting? I'll let the police know they need to watch Duane and see which direction he moves. South is where he might go when he hits Seattle. A lot of things can happen on a boat. Dee Anne will show. No doubt about it. She does hate him and always has. She followed him to Cancun. Let's hope he doesn't leave the Seattle area too soon. If he leaves Washington state, we might not be able to help."

A week later, they caught Dee Anne during the night with an empty gas can and an arrow bow slung over her shoulder. She was on the dock near Duane's new boat in the harbor at Tacoma. She pretended to be part of an archery team practicing night flares. She pointed to a boat the police knew belonged to their supervisor.

The smell of the gas also gave her away as did the colorful rag coming out of the open gas tank on Duane's boat. The police watching the new boat played poker and occasionally glanced at their computer screen.

The rag sticking out looked like a flag. They knew flags belonged on the back of the boat. Duane and his new girlfriend were a flaming arrow away from disaster.

Duane evacuated his boat, so the police bomb squad could remove the object. They wanted to check out the rest of the tank and the boat. They thought there might be a second device. Dee Anne put a second device in the tank toilet.

The judge came through with Duane's request for an annulment.

Dee Anne Fuller was charged with her many crimes and put in a different prison than Madeline Foster. She wasn't allowed to work near anything electrical, plumbing, or with fire. Neither woman would be free for a long time.

The cost of the investigation was huge. All the major players at headquarters in Los Angeles relaxed. The Chief congratulated his Captains. The Captains ordered catered food as congratulations to the detectives and the blue suits involved.

The streets were temporarily safe from Madeline and Dee Anne. Donnie was out of the fire business permanently. Mason was put in a jail cell with a snake charmer that killed a few people.

47 Case Wrap

Jonathan motioned Liam to come into his office. Hugh just left and looked at him in disgust. Liam didn't understand the hateful look.

"My birthday was last week. I shared my cake. What gives with Hugh?"

"Sit down, Liam. Congratulations to our best lead detective in the office. Thanks for wrapping up the high-profile Beverly Hicks's murder case and the rest of the murders. The discovery took a long time."

"I appreciate your praise."

"This is the final information given to the Chief. Plan 1 by Madeline Foster was stealing Duane Hicks's sailboat in Ventura. There were three women she knew named Connie Moore, Beth Sand, and Dee Anne Fuller. That plan failed and Duane decided to fly to Mexico for some fun. He mentioned the city and a bar he liked to Dee Anne who was the person who tipped him to the problem. Unfortunately, he didn't tell his wife where he was going nor report the incident to the police."

Liam knew this was the beginning of the end for Beverly Hicks.

"Next, Madeline and Beth got caught stealing a second larger sailboat and went to jail. Madeline sent Dee Anne to Mexico to find Duane. At this point, she had nothing to lose except a hunch. Money was a possible thought. We know Duane admitted telling Dee Anne about the insurance policies after his second date with her in Mexico. Dee Anne arranged for the dummy corporations to free Madeline. From there, things snowballed, and Plan 2 started."

Liam knew in some way Duane was very responsible. His boss continued.

"We know Madeline arranged the killing of Beverly Hicks while she was in jail. She felt the money was within her reach."

Jonathan turned the page.

"Along came Mason Jarett and Donnie Corwin. Mason read about Donnie's release and found him. I'm glad Mason confessed to killing Connie and Syd Coogan, aka Cougar, via gas and had Donnie burn the boat. Cougar beat him up a couple of months back for some money he owed him for boat repairs. Mason wanted to get even and lured him to his boat vowing to pay him. Connie came along. Mason saw a bracelet on Connie's arm and realized the two killed Beverly Hicks. Cougar brought out a gun and tried to kill Mason. Mason grabbed a board and hit them. If there was any remorse later for the killing of Connie or Cougar, Mason couldn't go to the police because he let Madeline stay at his place. The fool liked her and didn't know about Plan 1 or 2."

"Too bad Mason didn't go to the police before he used the gas. We could have used the information," said Liam.

"Madeline knew about Mason killing Connie and Cougar. She didn't care because there would be fewer people on her team to share the insurance money. Mason told us Madeline arranged for the snake to take out Donnie. Too bad we didn't catch Madeline at Mason's house. Next, we set a trap via a stakeout and caught Madeline Foster. She died at the scene after revealing her plans to one of our detectives. She threatened to kill Duane Hicks and Detective King. Madeline was thwarted by our own, Detective Knight."

Liam remembered vividly the scene.

"Dee Anne Fuller tried to torch Duane Hicks and his new girlfriend in Tacoma. The Seattle police working with Tacoma caught her. Dee Anne testified that Madeline was the leader of Plan 1 and 2. Dee Anne is in jail and awaiting trial. She will be charged for accessory to Beverly Hicks's murder, attempted murder of Duane and his new friend, and numerous other crimes. Mason Jarett is in jail for three murders and is awaiting trial. What a mess?"

"The case was a weird one. Mason and Donnie's involvement hindered our case in finding Beverly's killer. Beth didn't know much and was, therefore, out of the plans. Her landing in jail wasn't a problem for Madeline. We were thrown off track. We did finally get to the bottom of the case. Penelope and Hugh worked hard. They should also receive credit."

"I know they did, and they will. There will be bonuses."

Liam smiled. The Captain held up his hand.

"However, we have a current situation on our hands."

The smile on Liam's face went away.

48 Twenty Weeks – Decision

Liam wasn't sure he knew about the situation Captain Jonathan Harrison was talking about. He was just congratulated on the closed case and talked about receiving a bonus.

"I'm not aware of any new situation, sir."

The boss shoved a folder at him. Liam opened and read the document.

"I didn't realize the twenty weeks were over. The paper says she has the option to return to New York City. Penelope wants to return. Why? She hates the place. Her fiancé died. She was there on a stakeout and accidentally became a creep's hostage. The police were to blame for losing contact. Allan Duran found and saved her. He was shot in the line of duty. She shot the perp with her fiancé's gun. She did her job while he lay dying. I read the file."

Jonathan stared at his detective. Liam thought quickly. "Give her a promotion or more money."

Jonathan sat down and frowned.

"The file on Penelope King was closed. Is there some hacker you know that I don't know about? The last time we talked, you knew little other than Duran was a detective who died and was her fiancé."

Liam was caught.

"I talked with her dad when she got the silvered mirror piece in the neck. Penelope didn't want them to know, but she was wrong. Her dad was appreciative, and he sent me the file. We bonded."

"You bonded with Warren King."

GRAY AREA FOR A WOMAN

Liam felt he somehow betrayed Penelope.

"She doesn't know I read the entire file or that her father gave me the case file copy."

Jonathan was not going to be responsible.

"Liam, you never told me about Warren. I shouldn't be surprised. He's rich but a good guy. He loves his daughter to distraction. I tried to convince her to stay. Her father wants her to live in Los Angeles. They are thinking of buying a second condominium. More money didn't work with Penelope. I can't give her a promotion. She hasn't been here long enough. Tell her we don't have snow. She likes water. Use your talents, man."

Liam hadn't talked with Penelope since the incident at his home with Becka. He was busy with the Duane Hicks thing.

"She wants to leave. I can't stop her," said Liam.

Jonathan looked at him and quietly talked.

"The world is a crazy place. I talked with her before the end of this case. She was happy. Penelope was staying, and now she is leaving. There is a reason. The reason is not this case or the stakeout. Madeline didn't scare her. Something else scared her worse. You are to blame. Hugh told me that everything was your fault. That's why Hugh was upset."

Liam thought about the last scene with Penelope and Becka.

"I broke up with my girlfriend. Penelope, unfortunately, was there at my house. Her clothes were at the condo. It was probably my t-shirt that set Becka off. Things became misconstrued. The case took too long, and the living arrangement at the stakeout didn't help matters. Hugh and I should have done the stakeout together."

"Misconstrued? Liam, what is it with women and you? She is the third female who wants to leave this department. How do you get in so much trouble! I can't explain a third female leaving my office. This would look bad."

"Look, I never touched Penelope. Well, maybe a kiss or two when we went surfing and maybe again. They were friendly kisses. This happened before the stakeout."

Jonathan shook his head. "You don't do friendly. My head is on the line here. She has the day off. Fix this or you are out. Take a day."

"I'm out. Why am I out? You just told me I was the best lead detective."

"She's a better female detective and good looking. I'm sure she can lead the new female recruits that we will hire in the future and convince them to stay."

"I'm good looking since I bought a new shaver."

Jonathan steamed.

"Everyone in the department likes her. They don't like you. We don't want to lose her. Understand?"

"People like me. It's Hugh. He flips back and forth in his judgment."

Jonathan shut his office door and steepled his fingers together.

"Let me be frank. The Chief wants to give you a promotion, a new wooden office desk, a private office with a door, the brass name sign, and everything. I'll sign off but first please fix this."

Liam saw the new office being built. The office would belong to him. From the window glass, he would be able to see Penelope's desk.

Jonathan handed him the new brass nameplate.

"Your new badge is ordered per Kamilla."

"Oh, nuts."

Jonathan opened his door and left. Liam stepped out of his boss's office and sat down at his old desk. He put his feet on the wood.

Carter looked over.

"I like you, but sometimes you are too emotional about hating flowers."

"Cut the crap, Carter. Go out and watch Highway 405. I'm sure the fast traffic will be stimulating to your brain. No, wait, try the green sugar canister with your coffee."

Carter bent down and glared at him.

"Highway 405, come on!"

Carter went over to Penelope's desk and grabbed the plant food. He poured the green crystals from the canister onto Liam's desk. He put the canister down.

"I like Penelope better. She's at least nice. Get your stuff together before everything falls apart."

He shoved Liam's feet off the desk. The green crystals went flying. Liam watched miserably as Carter left. He brushed off the leftover plant food. He yelled.

"You are the one who is emotional."

The desk wouldn't be his for long. He touched the grooves in the wood made from his shoes. He opened and shut the desk drawer he fixed recently. The drawer felt apart.

"Not again."

Liam looked at Carter's desk. The desks were the same. He checked Carter's desk, and the desk wasn't locked. Liam pulled out Carter's drawer and emptied the contents. He took the electric screwdriver and put the bolt back on his old drawer. Then he thought about a better plan. The bolt was left slightly loose. He placed Carter's items inside and shoved the loose drawer into Carter's desk. Carter's drawer fit nicely in Liam's desk.

He whistled a tune and sat down.

"I'm the lead detective around here. Rank has its privileges. Let's see what falls apart."

He pulled the new drawer back and forth.

"New drawer works like a dream."

Liam returned Penelope's plant food to her desk. He touched her ferns. They did add ambiance to the office. He peeked through her ferns to make sure there was no one on the floor. Next, he put a sticky note on Hugh's desk.

"My drawer works fine."

Liam knew if Penelope left the department, they would have to hire a new detective. He didn't want to start over either. She was a good detective, and they worked well together. His boss was right to be upset. The boss hated change. Liam didn't want anything to change either.

"No wonder Hugh looked pissed. I've blown this whole partnership. I'm going to have to fix the issue."

GRAY AREA FOR A WOMAN

Liam took his electric screwdriver and placed the object in his car trunk. He wouldn't be needing the item at the office. He drove to the condominium. He rang her bell, and there was no answer. He parked his car in the visitor lot and talked with the security guard. The guard liked Liam. He told him Penelope took her surfboard out of the locked cage. Liam walked to the beach. He saw her.

Penelope was surfing. He went and sat on the beach. He watched. She looked great. Something was soothing about the way she controlled the board. He knew to control the board took great skill.

After an hour, she dragged her surfboard onto the sand. Liam was waiting for her. She saw him. Penelope dropped the board. She undid the leg tie. She didn't look exhausted.

"I'm on vacation. I don't need to talk to you until Monday."

"I can't go away. My boss wants to fire me because you are leaving. Why are you leaving? New York City isn't the answer. They have snow, and we don't. Trust me. Besides, we did nothing wrong. I wished we did something. But I respected you. We respected each other except for the kissing. The stakeout was scary, but we did it."

"Jonathan wouldn't fire you because I'm leaving."

"He would."

Penelope took off her neck cover and partially unzipped her wet suit. She looked toward the condominium building.

"The guard told you that I was surfing."

"He did. My shooting Madeline, saving your neighbors, and your life turned me into a hero."

"You are a hero. I'm sorry about our boss."

Liam approached. He was close. His hands rested lightly on her shoulders.

"This was not what I wanted to happen."

She looked at Liam.

"What did you want to happen?"

He suddenly realized. There was no confusion. All the nights and mornings they spent close together mattered.

"Why didn't you try something?"

She was waiting for him to answer and make the move. Liam smiled.

"I wanted you."

She searched his eyes.

"Too late. I'm leaving."

Liam took her in his arms. He knew the difficulty that happened with the other detective. She lost someone important. He wouldn't let her down. He planned on living for a long time.

"We can make this work. If you leave, I'll just follow."

Penelope hesitated.

"You would follow me to New York?"

"I'm not going away. I'm like the cord to your surfboard, attached in a good way. You looked great coming in. The wave was high. You are a real power woman. My woman."

Liam knew this was his big moment. He kissed her as if the world belonged to them. His confidence was catching. She put her arms around his neck and kissed him back.

"I love you," said Liam.

Penelope liked the look in his eyes.

"You are one hundred percent sure? We haven't kissed very much."

"Ten thousand percent at least. We can kiss more."

"I love you back. New York was bad luck. The more I thought about things, coming to LA was an escape mechanism. I came here for a change. Things happened. You happened. Another detective was not in the cards. I realize now that I was running from a relationship that became serious," said Penelope.

"You were serious about me?" asked Liam.

"Yes."

Liam felt the same. Every day they spent together brought them closer. They kissed each other again and again.

"Can we live together? I'm thinking in the same building, the same bed with matching pillows, scented candles, and seriously wide awake."

Penelope nodded.

"I can do matching pillows and scented candles. But I get to keep the fuzzy pajamas."

Liam thought about the pajamas. They weren't his favorite. He grimaced.

"We'll go shopping. I know a place that does romantic. You would look awesome in short bottoms and a romantic top."

A helicopter flew overhead. They looked and saw Dodge with his dog. Liam and Penelope waved. The helicopter came back.

Dodge was impressed with the couple below him. He punched a button, and Hugh's voice came over the console.

"They are kissing on the beach."

Hugh did a little dance in his backyard. He accidentally turned the hose and sprayed the hose over his fence into his neighbor's yard.

"You are sure?"

Dodge petted his dog as he looked at the young couple.

"I give them a month before he goes to the jewelry store."

Hugh couldn't believe what he was hearing.

"I have a new ladder," said Hugh.

Dodge chuckled.

"Signing off."

Hugh started singing loudly.

"Oh, Christmas tree, oh Christmas tree, wait until you see my twinkly bright lights."

His neighbor yelled.

"Pipe it down and drop that hose. What new ladder?"

Hugh was glad he complained to the boss at work.

"Now things can get back to normal."

He heard a loud crash next door. Something hit the cement driveway. Hugh turned off his hose. He tossed the hose next to the house.

"Roof shingles need replacing. That will cost my neighbor a penny or two. I think I'll be neighborly and bring over a macaroni hot dish. His wife likes macaroni. I can assess the damage."

Hugh yelled, "Emma, do we have any macaroni?"

His wife shook the macaroni blue box in the window for Hugh to see.

"Great. I might show him my new ladder. Nah, let the neighbor wait."

Hugh went inside and told Emma the good news that Penelope was staying in LA. He forgot to tell her about Liam and the kissing on the beach.

He poured the macaroni into the pan of hot water. Using some scissors, he cut the packet open containing the cheese. In twelve minutes, he was at his neighbor's doorstep with the casserole and rang the doorbell. The neighbor's wife opened the door and let him in.

49 Lights and More Lights

Liam, Hugh, and Dodge were hanging the lights on Hugh's house. They moved the new ladder.

Dodge commented, "This thing is lightweight but real sturdy."

Liam looked at the label.

"The ladder is some commercial brand with certification."

Dodge looked at the label.

"This ladder will withstand a fire. Great news, Hugh. Do you want to start a fire and test the metal?"

Hugh was glad his friends were visiting. They were close to normal.

"Naw, let's wait."

The women were with the kids finishing the tree ornaments.

"The outside lights aren't level," said Dodge.

Hugh responded.

"The whole house isn't level. Just eyeball it. Pop those screws in. The lights will float."

Liam took the electric screwdriver and finished the top of the home. He started on the next side. Dodge was behind him unwrapping the cord.

After three hours, the men were finished. Hugh was glad his two male friends did a good job. The lights weren't half bad. He went into the house leaving Dodge and Liam to put the empty boxes in the garage.

Liam stacked the boxes on a shelf marked Christmas. He showed Dodge the twinkle lights over the workbench.

"These twinkle lights were wrapped around a milk chocolate palm tree on Penelope's desk. The thing must have been two and a half feet tall. The DA sent her unusual stuff. Guess he decided the flowers weren't working."

"You are lucky, Liam because these lights are cool. I would have fallen for the man."

Liam slapped Dodge on the back.

"Heard you have a new office with a door," commented Dodge.

Liam smiled remembering the first day he walked into his new office."

"The desk is mahogany, and there's glass. The drawers work fine."

"I heard Carter's desk was having some problems. You wouldn't know about his desk drawer."

Liam rubbed his face and looked guilty.

"I thought so. He'll learn. Your old desk used to be mine. I hated that drawer with a vengeance. The glue didn't work either. I wish I'd thought about switching the drawers."

"Glue is expensive."

Dodge laughed.

"The promotion was a long time coming."

He rubbed Liam on the neck. They joined Emma, Penelope, and Hugh inside.

"You are sure our electric box is big enough to keep the lights illuminated?" asked Emma.

"We installed a generator solely for the lights. The electrician recommended the generator because the lights are on for such a short time and part of the year. There's a box with a button to remotely turn them on and off. No more climbing a ladder to plug in the light strings. This is better. Things should work great."

"Did you remember to get an authorization for the clear lights from the homeowner's association? Every time a house changes color on lights, you have to get new approval."

Hugh looked incredulously at his wife. He smacked his palm to his forehead.

"You mean I have to ask my neighbor for permission because I changed the color of the lightbulbs? He's on the board. That's pure nuts. I'm not going to ask."

Emma argued.

"I showed you the letter. The rule is new this year. Our neighbor pushed for the change. You must get permission."

Dodge raised his hand.

"I think Liam and I ought to visit the neighbor and get the okay on the lights. Hugh should stay home. Verbal works if you have two witnesses and a big dog. Hugh, why don't you flip the switch."

Liam looked doubtful about visiting the neighbor. Penelope encouraged them to go.

"We'll bake sugar cookies while you are gone. I'm thinking we need a double batch because of the bag of sugars, silver balls, and cinnamon hearts I brought."

The kids jumped up and down with joy.

Hugh picked up the remote gleefully.

Dodge and Liam went outside and knocked on the neighbor's door. The dog went along.

The neighbor opened his door and didn't recognize the two men. He backed away from the dog.

GRAY AREA FOR A WOMAN

He raised his hands in the air. He thought they were robbers. They explained the reason they were there. The neighbor slammed the door in their faces.

"He's downright unfriendly," said Dodge.

"I hate to say bad things about a person, but this one is a case called major rude."

The dog barked.

"Even the dog agrees with us."

Dodge walked off the neighbor's front porch and looked around.

"He has too many lights plugged into a single socket. This is a major fire hazard."

Liam looked.

"You are right. We might have saved his life."

The two men left and went back to Hugh's place. While they were putting frosting on top and eating cookies, the fire department trucks rolled into the neighbor's yard. They gave him the warning to remove his lights or be fined. His old lights were a fire hazard.

Hugh went outside and talked with the fire marshal. The fire marshal's wife was on the homeowner's association board. Hugh handed the fire marshal his request for a change in the light color.

A week later, the approval came in the mail. Emma was excited, and Hugh hit the switch again. All the lights burned brightly.

"This is beautiful. Our first Christmas will be with lights that stay lit. Thank you, Hugh."

50 Oysters, Decorations, and Dinner

Hugh wondered when his guests would arrive. They were late. Hugh looked over and saw Dodge and Liam installing lights on his neighbor's house. He walked over.

"What are you guys doing? This is enemy territory. You're supposed to be at my house installing my lawn decorations and eating oysters."

Dodge laughed.

"We're almost done. Don't worry. We're charging him three times as much. His wife hired us. We told her pink was in this year. They were the cheapest bulbs in the store. We told her we could keep the green ones. She's hated those green lights for years."

Hugh went back home. He didn't tell Emma.

The two men came over and slurped down oysters and crackers. The wooden snowman and Santa were out front installed securely on the lawn.

"They look perfect. Thanks, guys."

The two men left.

Two weeks later, on Christmas Day, Liam and Penelope, Dodge, and the dog were invited for Christmas dinner at Hugh's house.

The ham and a small turkey were cooking in the oven. The mashed potatoes were done on top of the stove. The gravy was ready. Green beans were waiting to be cooked. Pies were cooling on the kitchen table.

They all went outside to view the new light display on the house.

GRAY AREA FOR A WOMAN

"We do good work. They don't look crooked at all," commented Dodge.

"I staggered the hangars," said Liam.

"Works every time. Guys, we have lights and lawn decorations."

Everyone else agreed with Hugh. The lights were magical and festive.

They went inside and ate Christmas dinner.

While they were doing dishes, a group of people from the homeowner's association knocked on the neighbor's door. Dodge was outside with the dog and overheard the conversation. They gave the neighbor a hundred fifty dollar fine for not getting the proper authorization for pink lights versus the original green.

Dodge went inside. Hugh held the pie cutter.

"Anyone else here who wants a slice of homemade apple pie?"

The dog barked.

"Are you kidding me? What kind of dog eats apple pie?"

The kids took their partially finished plates of pie and put them on the floor.

"Dodge, your dog is spoiled," said Hugh.

Dodge grinned. She's pregnant.

"I like your kids, too. Thank you, Emma, for a wonderful meal and the pie."

Emma looked at her husband with pride.

"We might be able to squeeze in a puppy."

Hugh choked and sobbed.

"Not a puppy. They pee everywhere."

"We'd like a female," said Emma.

Hugh's eyes rolled, and he whined, "There'll be spots."

"Nothing a little fertilizer can't correct. You might have to buy a spreader," said Dodge.

Liam squeezed Penelope's hand.

"I'm glad you stayed."

"I wouldn't have missed this for the world."

A couple of helicopters buzzed over the house, and the kids ran outside with Hugh and Emma. They could hear the children shouting.

Liam looked at Dodge.

"Friends of yours?"

"I told them about the neighbor. He turned me in when I landed earlier this year. The fire people are friends. This neighborhood is outside the zone. It's considered a gray area. The fly-boys owed me a favor."

The helicopters flew over a second time and dropped tiny stuffed toys. The kids ran around the yard collecting them.

Liam took his fork and cut a piece of the pie. He gave the apple bite to Penelope.

Dodge petted the dog.

Liam looked at Penelope. The engagement ring on her finger sparkled. He also gave her a white bouquet for Christmas. Liam checked with her father.

"Mental note, she likes white roses."

When they left the Christmas dinner, the rain turned into light snow.

Liam took her hand and raced to their car.

"I know. I said it was warm here. This is an anomaly. Trust me."

"Trust you?"

GRAY AREA FOR A WOMAN

Penelope leaned over and kissed him.

Liam believed his evening was just beginning. He saw a shingle fall off Hugh's neighbor's roof.

"I thought the guy repaired the roof?"

His fiancée looked.

"Bad contractors. He didn't take Hugh's recommendation."

They drove home in slushy snow. When they entered the condominium, their Christmas tree looked beautiful. They chose multi-color lights.

He took her into his arms after she lit the candles in the wooden bowl. The room held a soft glow.

"Romantic and old-fashioned works for me."

Penelope felt wonderful.

51 Passion and the Rain

Liam looked at Penelope sleeping.

He slid out of their bed and went downstairs. He called her father.

Penelope awoke and picked up the landline receiver. She waited until the call ended, and she stepped out of the bed.

Her bags were packed from the prior evening. They were staying at Liam's house for a week. The car service was called. She was leaving.

Liam went to the guest bedroom and knocked.

"One minute and the egg sandwiches are ready."

He waited for three minutes in the kitchen. Penelope didn't arrive. He knocked on her door and pushed the door open when she didn't respond. He saw the note on the nightstand.

You told my father. I asked you not to tell my parents.

"Shit. She overheard our conversation."

Liam dialed her father. There was no answer. He sat waiting. Breakfast seemed to be over. The egg sandwiches were wrapped in foil and put in the freezer.

The doorbell rang. Penelope stood with a paper bag in her hand. Liam recognized the restaurant's name.

"The chef opened his restaurant. He allowed a special delivery when I mentioned your name."

"Special delivery is their specialty. The chef is a good friend. I've told him about my new detective. Penelope, you forgot your key. Come in."

GRAY AREA FOR A WOMAN

He let her pass.

Liam closed the front door and followed Penelope into the kitchen. She opened the bag and took a deep smell.

"This smells delightful, much better than eggs. The weather looks like rain. The sky is gray."

Liam looked outside. He took the package out of her hands and put the package on the counter. The sky certainly looked gray.

"I read your old case file. Your dad asked me about the current hostage case, and we talked about the mirror glass a long time ago. He was worried. I had to tell him because my detective job requires that I notify people. I'm your trainer and make the final call. Plus, they are part owners of the condominium that did get trashed."

She thought about his logic.

"We bonded."

"I can tell."

"I was afraid you left. What's in the bag?"

She looked at Liam. He approached. Penelope took him in her arms and touched his lips.

"Can't you guess?"

Liam kissed her. All he wanted in the world was in front of him.

"The rain will stop eventually."

"I know. To answer your question, the words are Kung Pau."

He understood.

"I love Kung Pau. We share."

"Always."

Liam kissed her with tenderness.

"I love you."

Penelope wasn't going to let him off so easily.

"We get married sooner."

Liam thought about their future.

"Your dad told me the same thing."

He put his head next to hers.

"Whatever you want, I'm in. We skip Greece."

Penelope could see the ocean.

"We should try surfing for one more time. There are places in Australia."

"We're talking big and scary waves. How about California?"

"San Diego?" asked Penelope.

"San Diego is close. The drive is beautiful. We could stop and eat fish. I know a couple of great restaurants."

Liam thought about the bruises from before. Some things were worth the pain. He remembered the kisses in the water. Penelope's kisses were worth the salve and bandages.

"We could go back to Lake Tahoe and curl up in a cabin."

"Now there's an idea. We can look for rentals online."

"Do you want the hot stuff now or later?"

Penelope looked wickedly at Liam.

He said, "Which hot stuff?"

Penelope's eyes were bright. He figured out what she was talking about. Food was not in her thoughts.

"Now is always better."

"I'll be gentle."

GRAY AREA FOR A WOMAN

He put the Kung Pau Chicken bag in the refrigerator.

Penelope raced upstairs. Liam was glad she returned. He took the steps two at a time.

52 Flight and Possibilities

Penelope turned into the parking spot that stated the words *Reserved.*

Liam looked at his fiancée.

"We should be at the main terminal. I've never been here."

Penelope opened the car trunk.

"We are in the right place. This is the private airplane terminal my dad likes to use."

She dragged her suitcase and walked toward an awaiting airplane. Liam grabbed his suitcase, locked the car, and followed.

On the plane, she told him to buckle up. Liam complied. Penelope fell asleep as soon as the plane was airborne. Liam ordered a drink from the person who asked.

The airplane landed on a small airstrip. Liam walked down the steps.

"Where's the terminal?"

Penelope joined him and looked at her watch.

"The limo should be here any minute."

Sure enough, a white limousine arrived.

"This is a rental?" asked Liam.

Penelope climbed inside. Liam followed her.

"My dad doesn't do rentals unless necessary when he is in Montana. Are you getting nervous about the wedding ceremony?"

"Your dad owns this machine?"

"Yes, and a couple more."

Liam processed the information.

"Really?"

Penelope told him the others arrived as planned. Liam knew Hugh and his wife plus Dodge were invited.

"They are staying on the ranch. We should see them shortly."

Liam was glad he would see someone he could recognize once the wedding party arrived."

"I didn't know."

Penelope felt bad.

"I should have prepared you better. The ranch is large."

Liam saw buildings appear in the distance. Penelope took his hand.

"You'll be fine."

"How big is the main building?"

She knew he would know soon enough.

"Twenty-two thousand square feet. There are four other cabins on the property for the workers and guests."

Liam rubbed his forehead. He looked around. The land went for miles. There were no other ranches in his sight. A headache was brewing.

"Do you want to back out?"

Liam knew he wanted Penelope. The package came with her. He would have to get used to her family on their turf. He waited a long time to find someone like Penelope. He was looking for someone, but she was a complete and amazing unknown delight.

"Never. Besides, we already bought the exquisite white dress with a beige satin tie."

Penelope and Liam worked with a designer to find the perfect gown and beige tuxedos for their wedding.

"Correct answer."

Liam stepped out of the limousine. He knew her parents weren't going to be there until later in the evening. He could familiarize himself with the territory. The maid showed them to their suite of rooms.

Penelope hugged him once inside.

"We can go for a ride later."

"On horses? Don't they bite? I probably should have checked my tetanus records," mentioned Liam.

Penelope suddenly realized he didn't know how to ride.

"City boy, I'll teach you to be a cowboy."

Liam looked worried.

"What is with the terrible face?"

Liam grabbed her and held her tight.

"I don't want to be a cowboy. You get rid of cowboys."

Penelope understood.

"I'll only teach you to ride a horse."

Liam kissed her.

"Is there a safe buggy?"

She shook her head.

"Yes, but you need to try a saddle. I want to take a picture for placement on my desk. We have gentle horses. They've been trained not to bite, except for *Lightning*. He's a handful. We do carry insurance just in case."

Liam looked doubtful. The last thing he needed on a visit to the ranch was a charged-up horse. Park him on the horse, and the chemical reaction would start. He wasn't riding a horse that might burst into flames.

Penelope frowned. She didn't know what was going through her fiancé's head.

"All our horses are the best breed my father could buy. There shouldn't be any trouble. You need to stop fantasizing about a disaster. Liam, I know this is not your territory, but it's mine. You are going to be safe. Trust me. Nothing exciting ever happens until we have guests."

"Guests are important. They might be what we need."

Penelope wasn't convinced by Liam's declaration.

"There will be good times between us."

Liam said, "The good times are around the corner."

Penelope nodded.

"I promise."

"No cowboy hat," said Liam.

Penelope was too wired up to argue. The whole wedding scene was also stressing her out. She went to her suitcase, found the object, and handed him a beige baseball hat. She also brought out one for herself. She threw a beige rain jacket at him. He caught the jacket. He noticed their hats contained a beige satin brim.

"Good, I'm glad we settled that issue."

Penelope knew their wedding day was going to be perfect.

Thunder sounded.

Liam shook his head. The sky was clear when they arrived. Penelope came prepared.

"Good thing we have a large barn."

He held her close.

"How did you pick Los Angeles for your next detective job?"

"I wrote my favorite cities on a piece of paper with separate sticky notes and numbers. I rolled the dice."

Liam shook his head.

"I was a roll of the dice?"

"Do you mind? I liked you immediately. The dice were my friend."

"The dice was fate or something else magical."

They heard Hugh banging on their door.

Liam groaned.

"Anybody in there?"

Penelope opened the door. Hugh walked in with Emma and Dodge. They wore the same hat and jackets. There also wore white buttons that read, *wedding party*. Liam looked at Penelope.

"My mom went shopping for the cabin guests in the wedding party."

Hugh stood with his hands on his hips.

"Liam, you shaved."

"Hugh, how about horseback riding. There's this cool horse called *Lightning*."

"You are a wise guy; Warren warned me about the horse."

Dodge intervened.

"I'll ride Lightning. We got acquainted this morning. He likes sugar cubes, but the apple fritter was the best."

GRAY AREA FOR A WOMAN

The five of them went to eat brunch before riding. When they were done eating, they stood in the large kitchen looking out the huge patio doors.

"I see purple," said Hugh.

Liam looked out the window. All he saw was fog.

Penelope watched her guests. She motioned Liam to step away. He followed her to their room.

"You are saved from riding. The fog will load with heavy dew. The others can play checkers. We can do other fun things."

Liam caught the fun part.

"I did see purple for a brief second."

"We have lots of lavender plants in the field. What you were seeing is something the locals call heather rain."

Liam liked the ranch layout and as far as he could see. The schedule showed him previewing the ranch after they were married. The schedule was a ride with her father.

"Something purple plus wet fog and rain. Interesting. Should I be worried about the ride with your father after we are married?"

Penelope looked at her calendar. There was no ride scheduled.

"I'll come along as an intervention."

Liam looked grateful.

53 Last Dance

Penelope adjusted the ruffled strap on her pink gown. The sheer ruffle went to the floor. She looked at her mother.

"This is too much for a dance party before my wedding."

Her mother assured her the dress was the latest fashion. Penelope didn't have any idea about fashion. She trusted her mother knew better. Warren banged on the door.

"Wendy, where's my daughter. I get the first dance with Pink."

Her mother opened the bedroom door. Her dad extended his awaiting arm and winked at her. Penelope went to the outdoor dance hall that was erected. Huge tents covered the back porch. She saw Liam smile when he saw her.

After dancing with her father to his favorite tune, Liam took over.

"I agree. Your mom can shop at any time for you. This pink dress is sexy and awesome."

A man tapped his shoulder. Penelope said the man's name, and Liam released her hand. The whole evening was ranchers and friends that knew Penelope.

The last dance started. Dodge beat Liam to Penelope. Dodge expertly ushered Penelope to the dance floor.

"You are a good dancer, Dodge. I never knew."
Dodge smiled.

GRAY AREA FOR A WOMAN

"Are you sure you want to marry Liam? I heard he was a lady-killer."

Penelope smiled.

"He told me the same thing about you."

"Guilty. I've known my fair share of women. You are in the top ten. I always go for a woman in pink."

"Good to know. I was going to pick the white version of this dress," said Penelope.

She saw Liam motioning to her.

"My fiancé is getting desperate."

Dodge twirled her around.

"Let him stew for a minute or two longer. I waited for my turn. I'm enjoying a dance with a pretty woman."

Penelope danced with Dodge.

"I can feel you need the last two minutes with Liam."

Penelope nodded.

"Thank you, Dodge, it is the last dance."

He bowed. Liam shoved Dodge out of the way. Dodge held his hands up.

"The dress is to blame."

Penelope knew the pink color was to blame.

"Next time, wear dull gray."

Penelope kissed her husband-to-be.

"I love you."

Penelope adjusted her pink strap.

"I love you back. Tomorrow, things will be too late."

Liam didn't care. He was all into the marriage.

"We dance tomorrow and run to our cabin after the first song. I'm not sharing you again."

Penelope knew the wedding dance tomorrow would be longer.

"Agreed. You liked my pink dress."

Liam was ushering her off the dance floor at a high rate of speed. Penelope took off her heels. They ran to their room. Liam shut the door and turned the lock.

Penelope looked into his eyes. There was no doubt in her mind.

The knock on the door surprised Liam.

"Champagne and a little chocolate, courtesy from Hugh and Dodge."

Liam opened the door, grabbed the cart, and ushered the cook's assistant out the door.

"Where were we?"

"Pink dress."

Liam looked at the ruffles.

"Where do I start?"

Penelope took a slow bite of the thick chocolate.

"The top."

Liam grabbed his girl. There was nothing more he wanted.

"I have to admit something," said Liam.

Penelope frowned.

"I was lost the minute you stood up at your cave, fern-like desk."

Penelope kissed Liam.

"I guessed. Your eyes gave you away."

Liam shook his head.

"It was the hesitation thing."

GRAY AREA FOR A WOMAN

"Dead giveaway," said Penelope.

Liam frowned. "I talked with Jonathan while you were getting dressed. He's leaving his vacation in Hawaii. There's been an arson fire in Los Angeles at a large warehouse complex. The Captain is putting Davidson and Carter on the case until we get back from our honeymoon."

"The fire department found the trigger for the fire?"

Liam was given a short version of the story.

"Explosives at the exits started first."

Penelope understood the police were looking for murderers.

"What's the other issue with the fire?"

"They found drugs in one of the warehouses and a lab. Some people were inside when the explosives blew. All six people died. They are in the process of identification."

"Turf war?"

"There might be a fight over territory. The police found no identification on the six people. There were lockers with money and keys but nothing else. No cars in the lot. The owner had no idea there was a lab in one of his buildings. Or so he claims. The security guards have disappeared. A month previous, one of the owner's other buildings was robbed of a shipment of expensive drones."

Penelope said, "There is a strangeness to this case."

"I think you may be right. The investigation could get sticky. There's a lot of money involved or rather a lot of drugs were enveloped by the fire.

Someone will need to pay. The insurance company will balk at sending checks for the building. They already paid for the insurance on the drones. The drugs aren't in the contract. The people might be where we have the most difficulty. Just a feeling of mine."

Penelope believed their work would be a struggle to unravel the fire and stolen goods. There could be multiple groups of criminals. Liam was a good detective. His instincts were sound.

"We'll have to hurry up and get married so we can return."

Liam said, "The fire investigation can wait. I don't care about the drones for the moment."

He looked at her dress.

"Where's the metal zipper? Don't the manufacturers put them in the back?"

He felt her dress, and there was no side zipper either.

Penelope guided his hand over the chiffon.

"A whole week for our honeymoon won't be enough, but we are taking the time away from the office. First, I must tackle this dress. There's no zipper."

She smiled.

"You'll need my help."

She was waiting for his agreement.

"Yes, Detective King, almost Knight."

She undid the hook.

Tomorrow he could use the last word. He found the hidden zipper in the front next to the ruffle. The zipper easily came undone. He nuzzled her long hair.

"Is it too early to call you my wife?"

GRAY AREA FOR A WOMAN

She stepped out of her dress. Liam helped her put the dress on a hanger.

"You'll have to call me Detective Knight in the office."

Liam took her back in his arms.

"Detective wife, I still need your help."

Penelope smiled exasperatedly. Liam was going to do his own thing with her name.

"The slip should be no problem. The fabric is stretchy."

"Stretchy? How about the rest of your wardrobe?"

Penelope kissed him.

"Wait and see, detective husband."

Liam went to the bottle of champagne and poured two glasses. He handed her a tall glass.

"I do."

Penelope was glad Liam said the words in private. They celebrated their upcoming marriage.

"I do," said Penelope.

Liam took her in his arms. "This is the best part of my day. The world and problems are locked outside."

"Mine, too. I do have a question. What changed your mind about our honeymoon location? We decided on Lake Tahoe."

"You kept staring at the Australia website after we chose Tahoe. I knew you wanted to go surfing. Even your parents knew. I figured things out when your mom sent you three swimsuits to my office. Water is cold in Tahoe and warm in Australia."

Penelope was astounded.

"My parents interfered. Why would they do that?"

"They love you. They wanted us to eventually share a hobby in California. I'm glad they did. The exercise will be great! We already have the condominium as a present. Your dad is buying a second unit."

Penelope hugged Liam.

"We can take the surfboard lessons together in Australia. I'll be close. I promise."

"I'm glad you said you would take lessons with me."

Penelope saw the fear disappear from Liam's eyes. He was deep and tough most of the time.

"I like you close."

Tomorrow would be wedding paperwork and cameras plus a large and super fantastic party.

GRAY AREA FOR A WOMAN

Author's List of Books

Knight Detective Series:
Book 1 - Gray Area for a Woman

Orange Carousel and Orchid Murders

Black Horse and Female Lawyer

Green Emeralds and Heist Club

White Boom and the Seagulls

Gold and the Spotted Jaguar

Raiment Red and a Raven
- A Southwest Mystery

A Wright Series:
Book 1 – Diamonds Blondes and Poison
Book 2 – Dead On Coordinates
Book 3 – Wild Golden Obsession
Book 4 – No Easy Target
Book 5 – Powerhouse Race
Book 6 – Cross Paths

www.ingramcontent.com/pod-product-compliance
Lightning Source LLC
Chambersburg PA
CBHW051241260626
47162CB00002B/553